OUT OF
Darkness

ALICIA PETERSEN

JOURNEYFORTH
Greenville, South Carolina

Contents

Chapter One

The day at school had ended. The other boys burst out of the synagogue doors in a group and ran off down the street. Elhanan watched them and heard their laughter echo from the gray stone walls. As always, the crowd of people in Jerusalem's streets was a colorful, jostling mass. None of them noticed him—a boy standing alone.

He reminded himself again that he was privileged to be a councilman's son. Yet there was pain in the privilege: his schoolmates shunned him. He admitted, too, that his attitude caused some of the isolation. But worry for his mother's poor health made him impatient with his schoolmates' frivolous interests and talk.

Elhanan started on toward home and drew comfort from the well-known streets. As he neared the city's edge, he also recognized many faces. The most familiar face among them belonged to a beggar—a blind Roman orphan boy about his own age. The two had struck up an unlikely relationship over the months.

He slowed his pace as he approached a major cross street. Then he peeked around the corner. The beggar boy sat on a worn stone step halfway down the block. He chanted an endless appeal, holding out his hand toward passersby.

Elhanan smiled. Their daily ritual was about to begin: a game in which he tried to pass Amplias without being detected. Leaning against a wall for support, he took off his sandals. The blind boy had so often caught Elhanan's passing that he felt the sandals must squeak. He tucked them under his arm, pressing them tight against his side. Then he stepped into the street where Amplias sat. As the distance closed between them, he moved more and more slowly, taking care not to disturb even a pebble. Amplias' chant continued unchecked. Elhanan tingled with the thought of winning. He was almost directly in front of the Roman boy's place on the step.

"Elhanan!" At the challenge Elhanan let out his held breath and dropped his sandals, admitting defeat. Amplias' sightless eyes looked straight at him, though they were aimed at chest level. Both boys broke into laughter, and Amplias crowed triumphantly, "How will you ever explain dirt from Jerusalem's streets on the *bottom* of your feet?"

Elhanan sat down beside the Roman boy and began putting his sandals on again. "You're uncanny, Amplias!"

The beggar shook his head. "The loss of one ability can strengthen another. But excuse me a moment. The hour is late, and alms have been few today." Amplias extended his open hand toward the passing crowd and chanted, "Alms for the blind. Please . . . coins for the poor blind boy."

Elhanan's heart hurt to see his friend beg. Had pagan gods caused him to be blind from birth? But no. He knew there were also Jews born sightless. He drew his legs tight up against his chest, wrapped his arms around them, and lowered his head onto his knees. Life was cruel to so many! The Roman boy had not yet completed thirteen years in this world, and yet he walked each day with awful hardship.

Amplias' voice broke into Elhanan's thoughts. "Why so quiet, my friend?"

"Forgive me, Amplias. As a friend I should bring joy to your day."

"Then share with me the sorrow of your heart, as well as its laughter."

Elhanan was silent a moment. Then turning his cheek onto his knees so he could look at his friend, he said, "Life seems so full of sadness! Why must there be cruelty and hurt?"

Amplias replied with equal thoughtfulness, "Those are questions asked endlessly, aren't they? But don't let my blindness weigh upon you. There are worse things! I might lack hearing, as well. Then I would—*could*—know nothing of the life around me here in the streets."

"But you shouldn't be here in the streets! You should have a home. You shouldn't have to sit here—"

Amplias gently interrupted, "You mustn't hurt for me. My life's not so hard as some."

"There you go again—refusing to rage or whine. But right here, on this street in front of us, are people fat with life's richness yet ever complaining. They are the ones who should suffer. But, instead, so often it's those who are good that are denied the goodness of life." He swallowed over the lump in his throat, then continued quietly, "I don't ask that just about you, but of my mother, also . . ."

"Ah, my friend. That's the real source of your pain, isn't it? These weeks of our game you've spoken now and then about her illness. Seeing her suffer, you suffer; and so you grow in tenderness toward others."

Elhanan flinched inwardly as the words struck home. "You're wise, Amplias, as well as good. How can you know so much, *see* so much in your darkness?"

"Things unseen by eyes may be plain to a sighted heart, eh? But enough about me. What news of your dear mother?"

"I wish I could report improvement. But there is none. She grows more pale . . . weaker every day."

"I'm sorry for the pain I hear in your voice. And yet—forgive me if I sound unfeeling—can't even the hurting cause you to be glad?"

Elhanan gaped at the beggar boy. "Cause me to be *glad*? How so?"

"Isn't there cause for joy just in having such a mother?"

The wistful note in Amplias' voice went like a spear to Elhanan's heart. How dare he whine before this one who had neither father nor mother? "You're right. I should look more at what I have than at what threatens. I'm a thoughtless fool, my friend. Forgive me."

Amplias shrugged ragged shoulders. "There's nothing to forgive. But you should go now, or your lateness will worry the very one of whom we speak."

Elhanan rose from the step, dusting the back of his tunic. "Until tomorrow, then, Amplias. I'll still find a way to pass without your knowing."

The beggar grinned, revealing startlingly white teeth. "Not so. These ears can't be outwitted!" As he spoke, Amplias tugged at a narrow leather thong around his neck, pulling out from under his tunic a small, smooth, oddly-shaped stone pendant. "See this? It stays always near my heart. And so the gods give me news of your approach."

Elhanan rose quickly, horrified by the sight of the pagan talisman. Bidding Amplias goodbye, he started on down the street, but his thoughts stayed in the beggar's world. The Roman boy had not only been denied sight; he had been cheated of family as well. His father was an unknown Roman soldier; his mother a camp follower. A child—any child—would have been unwelcome to such a woman. A blind child was a horror from which she had fled. But in spite of everything, Amplias was not bitter. Elhanan felt ashamed that his pagan friend's attitude more nearly reflected Torah precepts than did his, though he was son to a member of the Jewish Sanhedrin!

A vendor sitting cross-legged behind his wares called out "Hey, hey, Joseph's boy. Come see the pretties!" Elhanan stopped. "Tell your mama of these, won't you, eh?" The boy approached the vendor's low table, drawn by what lay across the old man's palm: a strand of smooth blue beads.

"You and your trinkets, Laban. How much do you want for them?" Elhanan spoke with forced casualness.

The old man's eyes disappeared among the wrinkles on his face, and his grin revealed great gaps between decaying teeth. "Ah, these are fine beads, young one. Only because I have a friend among the trader's caravan drivers could I obtain them."

Elhanan rose to the bargaining challenge. "Many must know your caravan friend, Laban. I saw beads like those in at least two of the market stalls."

The old man shook his head as he caressed the beads. "No, no, no, you saw none like these. Blue is seldom so rich! And notice the cutter's art here: how smoothly each bead has been turned. Feel them, young one. The hand can confirm what the eyes must surely see."

Taking the strand, Elhanan reveled in the beauty of the beads. As the sun shone on them, they seemed to capture tones of the sky itself. But he kept his eyes lowered, not wanting Laban to see his pleasure and use it for bargaining advantage. So he shrugged and handed the beads back across the table. "Much indeed like those in the market, Laban. But—only out of curiosity—what price are you asking?"

The old vendor pursed his lips. "Price? Hmph. It's beyond your reach . . . or your deserving." The old man busied himself over his wares, packing up in exaggerated haste. But he left the beads lying on a square of cloth. "The day draws to a close, and weariness makes me simple. Such a special strand must go to some rich

Roman lady. Several stop by my place here on the street. They know that old Laban offers quality goods."

"You flatter yourself, Old One. The Romans pick over each caravan's goods as soon as they reach the city. They don't need to wait until your trinkets appear here." Then Elhanan pretended to shift his focus. "What of this brass incense pot?"

Laban was not fooled. "Incense pots, as fine as mine even, are not worthy of your mother. I remember her from days before her illness. But these beads . . ." his hand stroked them lovingly, "these would give her great delight. Think of bringing this, the heavens' own blue, into her sickroom. Imagine her pleasure in having them about her neck."

Elhanan winced. It was as if the canny old vendor had read his mind. At first sight the boy's heart had fastened upon the beads as a perfect gift for his mother. He badly wanted to do something special to encourage her. He had only given her gifts purchased by his father. But that was childish. He was in his thirteenth year. Childhood was ending. He should assume responsibility that befitted his years. He wanted something to be his *own gift* to her. But here at Laban's vending table he must mask his intentions. "Don't you think my mother has blue beads aplenty? It would be no great gift to add another strand."

Laban chuckled with genuine delight. Bargaining was his favorite part of selling. "Heh, heh, heh. Blue is blue, and beads are beads, except in *special* cases like this. If your mother saw this strand, she would throw any others to the crows. To the crows, I tell you!"

"You caw like a crow yourself, Old One. But you can't lure me with your pretties." Elhanan made himself turn away.

Laban cackled again and rattled the beads. "Hey, hey, hey. Don't walk away from these beauties, Joseph's boy." The sound of the beads drew Elhanan like insects drew fish in the garden pool at home. He turned back toward the vendor again.

"I must walk away, and quickly, or my mother will worry. Will you tell me a price, or no?"

"Now, now, now," Laban protested. "Of course I'll tell you the price: thir—twenty shekels."

"Impossible!" Elhanan felt great disappointment. How could he ever hope to get so much? The vendor rose and came out from behind his table. Moving with his lifelong limp, he came close to Elhanan.

"Yes, yes, yes. The price is impossible . . . for me! For anybody but you, I'd ask thirty or even thirty-five shekels. And anyone who knows quality would pay gladly!"

The sincerity in Laban's voice surprised the boy. The vendor was not bargaining or bantering. "I believe you, Laban, and I thank you. But twenty shekels. There's no way I can get—"

"What of your father, boy? Eh?" Laban squinted at him against the westering sun.

"I'll not ask him. I mustn't, anymore."

"Heh, heh. It's as I thought, then, eh? I've sensed it as you've passed my table here in the street these months. The boy in you grows smaller, and the man yearns to take his place. Is that it, eh, Joseph's boy?"

"I—" To his embarrassment, Elhanan's throat tightened with emotion, cutting off his words.

"Now, now. Never mind. We'll make a pact, you and I. Man to man. Payment can be made a bit at a time. These beads will be yours, when you complete their stated price."

"No, but—"

The old man silenced Elhanan's protest with a raised hand. "Enough of talk now, boy. You should be able to gift your mother with these special beads, all of your own earning. So it's done. Decided. There'll be no great hurry on my part, nor worry on yours. Just work, and save, and bring to me as you're able. That's all you need do to get you these."

"Not me; my mother."

"Ay, ay, so I meant to say. But worry won't get her the beads either. Only effort, and growing, and purpose. So, so, so. Do we understand one another, eh?"

Elhanan could only nod, he was so full of gratitude and excitement. Laban clapped his hands in satisfaction. "Good. So we are agreed, young one! And come look at the beads whenever you want—to remind you of your goal, eh?" Elhanan watched while the old vendor wrapped the necklace in its square of protective cloth and tucked the packet into a leather pouch he wore concealed under his left arm. The fact that Laban concealed the beads so carefully made their value evident.

Elhanan's heart began to sing as he moved on down the street. His head filled with schemes for earning twenty shekels. Blue. The beads were so blue. Like his mother's eyes.

But as suddenly as his heart's song began, it stopped. Rounding a final corner he could see his house halfway down the street. It was a sturdy, welcoming home, its large size indicating the Councilor Joseph's social status. But between Elhanan and home lay terror. A loud, rough voice assailed him.

"So there he is at last. Elhanan. El*hay*nan. Womany and weak El*hay*nan! You're late today, aren't you?" Maachah stood squarely in the way, his feet planted wide apart, arms crossed. Elhanan felt cold as he looked into Maachah's strange gray eyes, but he squared his shoulders and willed his trembling legs to move forward.

Though he was only two years older than Elhanan, Maachah was much larger in size, and he had chosen Elhanan as a target for bullying. He deceived his Councilor father and other adults by acting humble and obedient while in their presence. But whenever he was free from supervision he delighted in terrorizing anyone or anything that came to his notice.

As Elhanan drew closer, Maachah took up a familiar theme. "And how was school today, oh Wise One?"

"Fine," Elhanan answered through clenched teeth.

"How's that? Speak up. Surely the Rabbi insists that you speak clearly. Again. How was school today?"

"F-fine."

Maachah howled with delight. "*F-fine*?" he mocked. "But what more could be expected from a tongue as weak as its owner?"

Elhanan had drawn abreast of Maachah. But as he tried to pass, the older boy tripped him. He fell roughly to the cobbles and winced in pain, but he refused to give Maachah further satisfaction by crying out.

"Tsk, tsk. How very clumsy you are today, oh scholar! Here, do let me help you." With that, Maachah grabbed Elhanan's elbow and, while pulling him to his feet, purposely dragged him across the stones. Fighting back tears, Elhanan retrieved the things he had dropped, then gratefully moved beyond Maachah's physical reach. The bigger boy's lashing voice, however, continued to bombard him.

"Goodbye, El*hay*nan. Sleep well, El*hay*nan. May we meet again tomorrow, Mouse!"

Elhanan carefully measured his pace until within the gated wall of home. Then he broke into a run. His mother would be waiting, concerned about his late return. But he didn't want her to see the blood on his knees. He hurried to the fishpond which lay to one side of the garden. He scooped up water and rinsed away the blood. The pond became a small cauldron of activity as the fish responded to a supposed feeding. Drying his knees on poolside leaves, Elhanan spoke softly toward the water, "I'm sorry, my friends. You have to wait. I'll bring your food out later."

"Elhanan? Is that you?" The call came from the house, the voice round and full like its owner. Elhanan quickly picked up his belongings and hurried toward the house. He found the doorway filled by Leah, who was frowning fiercely. "You know you're late, of course? You've made your poor mother concerned." Though he felt rightly rebuked by the words, he felt no dread of the speaker, for she was like a grandmother to him.

"I'm sorry, Aunt Leah. I was . . . um . . . detained. I'll go right away to Mama."

"See that you do. Then make a return visit to me, and I might give you a little something to see you through until time for the evening meal." Leah removed her bulk from the doorway, allowing Elhanan to enter. As he passed into the cool interior of the house he smiled, thinking how very much Leah resembled a large ball. Round in both face and body, she was full of faithfulness and caring. The whole, however, was overlaid with gruffness. Elhanan had often thought she purposely hid her soft heart lest others take advantage of her. He knew, too, that Jerusalem's merchants held her in high esteem for her ability to judge quality and for her determined but fair bargaining.

Leah was not his real aunt, nor was her husband, Uncle Tobias, his real uncle. They were servants. But in a long-ago Year of Jubilee they had chosen lifetime service over freedom. So each of them had an ear on which the lobe had been pierced by an awl. The servant-family relationship in the household was one of mutual affection and gratitude. Joseph often pointed out to Elhanan that Leah and Tobias were a great gift from Jehovah. The full value of that gift had become unmistakably clear when Rachel fell ill.

Elhanan paused outside his mother's room. He drew a deep breath and pulled down the hem of his tunic, making sure it covered his battered knees.

"Mama?" he spoke into the semidarkness.

"You're late today, Elhanan." Her soft, melodic voice sent a pang of regret to his heart. "But I don't mean to chide. Though I long for your return from school each day, I wouldn't deny you time spent with your friends. The young need the young."

Elhanan wondered what his mother would think if she knew his sole friend to be a Roman beggar boy. "You know I like best to be here at home, Mama," he assured her.

"You're a dutiful son, Elhanan. Tell me now of your day." He sank onto the bedside stool. Avoiding his mother's eyes, he gazed hard at his hands, forcing his thoughts back to the unremarkable happenings of the school day. "Rabbi Beninu wasn't feeling well. He was sneezing and coughing throughout our lessons, and he sounded like this." So began Elhanan's usual recital of happenings in the larger world outside his mother's confined one. He knew how she treasured reports of even the simplest things he and his father brought home. They seemed to strengthen her grip on life—a grip that grew weaker each day. And so he rattled on, liberally embellishing his tale. It was well worth the effort—his mimicry and colorful commentary made his mother smile.

By the time Elhanan finished his recital, however, Rachel was noticeably tiring. She reached out to ruffle his hair. "It gives me joy to share another of your days, my son. Now I must rest so I'll be able to join you and your father for the evening meal." Her eyelids fluttered closed.

As he quietly left the room, he visualized Laban's beautiful blue beads. He must get them for his mother! The lovely stones must lie about her slender neck, echoing the rare blue of her eyes. Fear squeezed his heart as he thought, "Mama may not live even to her natal day. I must get her the beads. I *must*!"

Chapter Two

Elhanan, his mother, and his father had finished their
evening meal and gone out of the house into the garden.
This was his favorite time, his favorite place. The family had
observed day's end quietly like this for as long as he could remember. He felt sure his mother had begun the tradition. He
looked at her now. She and Joseph sat side by side on a carved
stone bench. Rachel looked as frail as a child beside Joseph's
masculine good health. Elhanan enjoyed watching his father and
mother together. Because he had overheard conversations and
noticed the behavior of other married couples, he knew his parents' love bond was rare.

The paleness of Rachel's skin was even more apparent here
than in her darkened room, yet the boy sensed that his mother
drew something essential from the garden.

"Elhanan, I see your work with the lichen have been successful. The plants are growing well." His mother smiled as she spoke. He flushed with pleasure at her words.

"Yes, Mama. They're taking sturdy hold. Wait—I'll let you see one more closely." He carefully picked up one of the small rocks that bordered the fishpond. Rising, he took it to Rachel. Her hand moved lightly over the delicate green moss that topped the rock.

"It makes a royal cloak, doesn't it, Joseph? Who but our Elhanan could coax the lichen's quick adaptation to its new home."

Joseph smiled at wife and son. "You've taught him well, Rachel. Under your guidance he and Tobias are keeping the garden healthy. And soon you'll be well and again able to care for these and the other plants you love."

An expression of pain appeared in Rachel's eyes. "I yearn for that, Beloved. But should Jehovah choose otherwise, I don't . . . ."

Joseph slipped an arm around his wife. She returned the lichen-clad rock to Elhanan, then leaned against Joseph, who said, "Surely Jehovah's choice is to return you to full strength. We pray each Sabbath for that, don't we, Elhanan?"

Replacing the rock at poolside, Elhanan forced assurance into his response. "It's our most earnest petition, Mama. Father and I both feel Jehovah hears and will answer."

Rachel smiled. "I'll rest myself, then, in your prayers. Ahhhh . . . Was ever woman more richly blessed than I in having the two of you! But now I must rest. Perhaps tomorrow I'll be able to spend longer here in the garden with you."

"You seem a bit stronger every evening, my love. Why—within a very few months we expect to see you active here in the garden just as you used to be. And now let me help you in so you can rest." Joseph gathered his wife into his arms, lifted her effortlessly, and moved toward the house.

Elhanan called after them, "It's so, Mama! Within a very few months." As his parents disappeared into the house, he thought about the request to work he planned to present to Joseph. He silently thanked Jehovah for his father's mention of the coming months. Somehow, that reference to time's passage validated the pressure he felt about wanting to earn his own money to buy his mother the beautiful blue beads.

Joseph returned to the garden. Glancing up, Elhanan noted the change so evident lately in his father. It was as if he wore a cheerful mask in his wife's presence. Now, with Rachel gone from the garden, his shoulders sagged, and his step was listless. He came to stand near where Elhanan knelt removing weeds from around the base of a small tree. Joseph's voice was weary when he spoke. "Your mother is right, Elhanan. Your hands, like hers, have the gift of nurturing life. Had I attempted caring for the garden when she fell ill, nothing would have survived."

"She praises me too highly, Father. I do only what she taught me."

"The garden thrives while she who planted it wilts!" Joseph's voice rasped as he turned away.

Elhanan rose from his knees and touched his father's arm. "Jehovah *will* answer our petitions for Mama won't He, Father?"

Joseph pulled himself erect. He laid his hand on Elhanan's shoulder. "Forgive this faithless father, my son. I spoke from the emptiness of human sight. Instead we must tap into the fullness of the Law and the Prophets. Let's claim together the great promise from Jeremiah: There Jehovah tells us to call Him, and He will answer. In His answer will be great and mighty things that are beyond our comprehension."

As the words of promise sounded in the gathering twilight, both father and son felt lighter of heart. Elhanan knelt again to his weeding.

"Father, you spoke earlier of coming months, and of the healing they may bring to Mama. I . . . I want to do something special—soon—for her."

Joseph moved slowly toward the stone bench. "Special? How so?"

"Old Laban the vendor has a necklace in his wares. It's far finer than the things he ordinarily sells."

"Of what sort is this necklace, Son?"

"The stones are rarest blue, Father. They've been smoothed perfectly, and they're carefully matched."

"I know the type piece you describe. If the stones and working are fine, the price will be high. You wish me to purchase this necklace for your mother? Is that what you have in mind? If so, I'll need to inspect the necklace myself."

"No. I don't mean for you to do it, Father. But me. I wish to give the necklace to Mama myself."

"Yourself? But the cost! What price is Laban asking?"

"Twenty shekels. But he says he could get more. And . . . well, I believe him, Father. It's as if— I think Laban wants me to have the beads for Mama."

Joseph's reply was thoughtful. "Hmmm. Old Laban enjoys a reputation for honesty on the street. Still, I'll stop by his stall one day soon. But to the point. If the piece is as fine as Laban claims, and the price fair, how do you propose to pay for it? Would you have me loan you the money?"

"No, Father. I want . . . er . . . I must . . . purchase the necklace myself. I want to use money that's not on loan, but earned."

"Ah, I see." Joseph was silent a moment. "It's an honorable intention, Elhanan. A manly one. I see in it that your heart keeps pace with your body's growth. That pleases me. Shall I inquire among my friends?"

Although he recognized the benefit of his father's offer, Elhanan replied, "Thank you, but no. This gift, all of it, must be my own. I'll ask in the streets and the marketplace until I learn of some opportunity for employment."

Joseph nodded his understanding. "I'll be honest, Boy; it's not easy to see you approach the doorway into maturity. It seems to come too soon. Yet at the same time I delight—"

Joseph stopped speaking, interrupted by Tobias' hurried entrance into the garden from the house. "Master, Councilor Nicodemus and his daughter have come to visit. Do you wish to come inside, or shall I ask them to join you here?"

"Bring them to the garden. Our visiting here will mean less chance of disturbance for Rachel. Thank you, Tobias."

Elhanan chuckled inwardly, thinking that just as Aunt Leah resembled a ball, Uncle Tobias could be likened to a stick; a short one at that. The tiny man and his oversized wife, though laughably different physically, nevertheless were strangely similar. He had mentioned that fact some days earlier, to his mother. She had responded by pointing out that their likeness to each other came from long years of living together. He remembered her words: "It's that wonderful, total unity Jehovah intended for man and wife, my son. It does not come quickly or easily; nor does it always come at all. But its reality brings delight not only to the couple themselves, but also to the heart of Jehovah." Elhanan sighed as he remembered the conversation. It had been one of those moments in which he more clearly recognized his mother's quiet wisdom and her contribution to every area of his life. Surely Jehovah would not let her illness continue to grow worse until it ended in death.

Nicodemus bustled into the garden. Close behind him came Adina, his daughter. "Ho, my friends!" Nicodemus exclaimed.

Joseph rose to welcome the visitors. "Come be seated here with me, Nicodemus. Adina, you no doubt prefer Elhanan's company to ours."

The two men sat down and fell into conversation. Adina and Elhanan moved in friendly silence toward the fishpond. Adina smiled as they knelt on the ground beside the pool. "All the way here Father has been mumbling, 'Whatever would we do without our friends, Adina? How ever could we escape your stepmother's tongue?' Poor Father. Mother has been—"

"In one of her *Terror Times*?" Elhanan finished the thought for her. Adina's real mother had died while the girl was barely old enough to walk. Pashura, Nicodemus' second wife, had a difficult personality, and she was unstable in her emotions. As a result, their home was often tense and unhappy.

"Yes. Mother has been awful for days now." Adina went on to describe her stepmother's most recent unpleasantness. He only half listened, because the story was always basically the same. Pashura was voicing selfish demands for something or other, making her husband and stepdaughter miserable.

Though unable to hear much of the men's conversation, Elhanan caught enough to know his father and Uncle Nicodemus were talking about the man named Jesus. The strange Nazarene had been much discussed in their family and with friends ever since Joseph and Nicodemus had sought out the fellow late one night months ago. Elhanan's mind moved on to contemplate the man Jesus all over again. Both his father and his Uncle Nicodemus had described a very ordinary man. There had been nothing to distinguish him physically from any of the others gathered there in Simon's house.

But what strange words had come from the Nazarene's mouth!

Except a man be born again he cannot see the kingdom of God. His statement had repeated itself over and over in Elhanan's mind through all the months since his father had quoted it. *That which is born of the flesh is flesh, and that which is born of the spirit is spirit.*

The puzzling statements made by the Nazarene not only remained with Elhanan, but with his uncle and his father as well. In fact, both Joseph and Nicodemus were searching their Scripture scrolls trying to reach a conclusion about Jesus' identity and his message. Their search for understanding was becoming more difficult as the Nazarene's popularity grew and opposition mounted against him.

Elhanan's thoughts suddenly came back to the present. Aunt Leah appeared in the doorway. She moved carefully, carrying a laden tray. Uncle Tobias followed close behind her with a small stool. She stopped before the two men and nodded toward a spot just in front of them. Her husband moved forward and placed the stool as she'd indicated, then he returned to the house. Aunt Leah balanced the tray on top of the stool. As she began to pour cool goat's milk into four silver cups, Tobias returned carrying basin, ewer, and towel. Beginning with Nicodemus, the old man poured water over each person's hands, catching the overflow in the basin; he then offered the towel.

After washing their hands, Elhanan and Adina claimed their goat's milk and fat purple grapes from the tray, then they again moved a short distance from their elders, this time to sit on a vine-covered rock outcropping. Leah and Tobias began lighting several small clay oil lamps that were in various places about the garden. Elhanan leaned against the rock face, and as he watched Aunt Leah, he thought the lamp flames resembled small bright flowers blooming against the oncoming darkness.

Adina looked up from the grapes in her hand. "How go your studies, Elhanan?"

He made a face at her through the twilight. "Most days my studies don't seem to go at all; they lie lazily in one place—like old dogs in the street."

Adina moved restlessly. "Still, Elhanan, you have the opportunity for school. How I wish it were possible for me to attend synagogue school! But we girls have no such choice."

Mimicking her tone, Elhanan replied, "But you—among girls—do have special choice."

Adina laughed. "Yes, you're right. Though I'm sure he wishes he had a son, Father generously encourages me to study. But still, you're free to come and go. You get to discuss what you're learning with classmates and teachers."

"Your picture of synagogue school is too colorful, Adina. It's not realistic. And as for coming and going, that can mean running the gauntlet of Maachah's jibes!"

"Maachah! Is he still bullying you?" Adina's voice was indignant. "Why don't you tell your father?"

"Only a child runs to its parent and begs for protection. I want to . . . I *must* become strong enough to defy Maachah."

Adina's dark eyes snapped with anger. "But Maachah is heavier in weight and older in years than you. And he's filled with brute cruelty!"

Joseph's call to them ended the uncomfortable discussion. "Elhanan, Nicodemus tells me their visit must end. You and Adina will have to continue your talk at another time."

The four friends bade goodbye, and Uncle Tobias appeared from the house to usher Nicodemus and Adina out the garden gate.

Joseph and Elhanan began moving toward the house, but they stopped as the boy posed a question. "Father, Adina speaks often of her regret that girls are not allowed to attend synagogue school. Yet when we talk, it's clear that her learning under the private tutor Uncle Nicodemus employs is much on a level with our synagogue lessons."

Joseph responded thoughtfully. "I'm glad Adina has opportunity to study, since she desires it. Your mother had a similar upbringing, and I've been grateful for what that has meant in our years together. As you go on through life you'll observe great variations in mental keenness in both men and women, Elhanan. I believe, however, that the important thing is to ascertain the heart behind the mind. Coldness or pride in either woman or man makes the mind a cruel, cutting thing—and therefore a misused gift."

The two walked on again, Elhanan lagging behind to consider what his father had said. Joseph opened the door to the house. As he stepped into the lighted interior, his shadow fell long behind him. Seeing it, Elhanan knew joy in being, as in old Laban's words, "Joseph's boy."

Chapter Three

One morning as Elhanan and his father broke their night's fast together, Aunt Leah contributed to the conversation. She was both excited and assured as she spoke. "Tobias discounts the tales, Master. He says my cousin's mind has deserted her. But Iscah has always been the soul of common sense."

Iscah was not a stranger to the household. She was the only one of Aunt Leah's relatives ever to visit Jerusalem, and she had come several times over the years. Remembering her stolid bearing and ponderous speech, Elhanan doubted that she could imagine anything.

Uncle Tobias snorted. "How much common sense can be credited to one who has spent her entire life in Nazareth, of all places."

Aunt Leah's reaction was vehement. "Nazareth is our own birthplace, Tobias! Master Joseph's kindness has made us residents of Jerusalem these years. Still, our Nazarene roots should not be disparaged; it's disloyal to—"

Joseph spoke to forestall a marital spat at that point. "Enough, you two. You'll wake your mistress. Now, Leah, tell me again what your cousin told of this Nazarene—this Jesus."

Triumphantly, Leah settled herself to relate what she had heard. "There are too many wonderful things to relate at one time, Master. Iscah was so instantly taken with the fellow's person and power, and so upset because the villagers drove him away, that she and some of her friends began to follow him from place to place. She spilled out tale after tale."

"And these were tales of *miracles*, Leah?" Joseph's tone was thoughtful.

"Miracles indeed! Healings! Demons cast out."

Leah's recounting of her cousin's experiences in following Jesus about the countryside so interested her hearers that Elhanan had to hurry toward synagogue school to avoid being late. *Healings . . . Healings.* The word echoed and re-echoed in his mind. Could it be true? There was more and more talk of such things done by the man Jesus. Might there be someone, perhaps Jesus—someone in this day—to whom Jehovah gave the power to do what Iscah claimed to have seen—people freed from deafness, from crippled limbs, from . . .?

Suddenly the boy found his way blocked, and his mind abruptly came back to the present. He had been so deeply in thought he'd not noticed that the crowds in the street around him had grown quiet, that those who would normally be moving were, instead, standing still. He had pushed unheeding through the throng, until all at once he came up hard against a Roman pike held as a barrier.

The tall, muscular Roman soldier holding the pike glowered down at Elhanan, "Get back there, Jew boy! Such mindlessness may get you into trouble one day—trouble such as *this*." On the last word, the soldier clamped a hand on Elhanan's head and pressed his chest hard against the restraining pike. Then he forced

the boy's head forward, twisting it to make him face to the right. At first the shafts of morning sun slanting down into the street dazzled Elhanan's eyes. Then forms took shape, and he saw a group moving slowly toward where he stood held motionless by the Roman's iron grasp. The group was made up of men: five prisoners urged and whipped forward by a small contingent of Roman soldiers. Each prisoner struggled to carry a great beam of wood. Their heavy ankle chains rattled on the cobbles. Crucifixion. These men were on their way to be crucified!

Elhanan's head spun; bile rose to the back of his throat. With a tremendous exertion of will, the boy fought off nausea and weakness. He tried to close his eyes against the sight before him, but horrid fascination kept them open. It seemed an eternity before the awful procession had passed, until the soldier released his head and shoved him against a wall, until the crowds slowly returned to normal movement and speech. Elhanan continued to lean against the wall where the Roman had flung him, oblivious of his physical pains. He was consumed with inward hurt, anger, and hatred made knife-sharp by helplessness. All his life he had heard those emotions expressed by the adults around him in the Jewish community. But only at this moment did he understand in the personal sense. Rome. Rome was a monster putting a crossbeam of suffering on the back of every Jew and chains of captivity upon the ankles of his people. Why? Why must it be so? How long would such miserable slavery continue? When, oh when would Jehovah fulfill His promise to free them from the burdens, the chains, and the whips?

Tears stung Elhanan's eyes as he resumed his way through the streets to school. He felt a great reluctance now to get there and begin the day's lessons. Because of what he had just seen in the street, he knew the rabbis' pleadings for the students to patiently endure would sound more hollow than ever.

"Elhanan? Your step is slow today. Are you ill?" It was Amplias, and the Roman boy's words brought Elhanan to an abrupt halt. He dropped to sit beside his blind friend. But his emotions were so intense, so tangled, that it took some time before he could speak. The Roman boy resumed his begging litany, thereby offering Elhanan the gift of privacy.

At last Elhanan was able to break his silence. His tone was flat. "Today I envy your sightlessness, Amplias. You don't have to see the ugliness that walks Jerusalem's streets."

"What is it that you've seen, my friend? Do you care to tell me?"

Elhanan hesitated, reluctant to voice his hatred of Rome to Amplias, a non-offending Roman. But he knew his friend's wisdom, and he trusted his ability to comprehend the emotional conflict between personal friendship and national enmity. So, slowly, Elhanan described the scene he had just been forced to watch, and he expressed both his anger against Rome's tyranny and his longing for Israel to be freed from it.

"You've seen an ugly picture, and of course your heart hurts because of it." Amplias paused, then he went on more slowly. "The longing of which you speak, for freedom and the hope for peace . . . those lie within each of us, don't they? Longing and hope. Strange, but I've lately heard whisperings of both here in the streets. There's talk of a healing prophet going about the countryside. It's said he frees bodies from crippling and disease, but that he also claims the power to free souls from hopelessness."

"If the one you mention hails from Nazareth, my Aunt Leah just this morning was telling wondrous tales of him. A relative of hers claims to have witnessed some of his miracles."

"Yes, that's the fellow—a Nazarene. And there is a word sometimes spoken in connection with the stories of his doings—the word *Messiah*. I don't know if it's part of the man's name, or . . ." Amplias' voice conveyed a question.

"*Messiah* is not really a name," said Elhanan; "it's a title meaning Anointed One. Our prophets wrote often of such a one—one who will come to free Israel and to give our people a kingdom marked by peace and love."

Amplias sighed. "He's to do that only for Israel?"

Elhanan drew his brows together, contemplating Amplias' question. "Well, the prophecies, of course, are addressed to Israel. And yet, how could peace and love really be said to reign if they only extend to one nation? Your question is a good one, but I can't answer it. I'll ask my father. He studies the Torah every day. But as for the present situation: this man—Jesus by name—this man can't be the Promised One."

"Why such surety?" Amplias asked.

Elhanan blushed at the challenge, but he replied confidently, "Because he comes from Nazareth! Nazareth is an unimportant, miserable village that's held in contempt by our people. No king could come from such a place!"

Amplias responded softly to his friend's assertion. "No king such as you and I picture in our minds. But how accurate are imaginings? A king who is able to replace human strife and hatred with peace and love would have to be a very different kind of king, wouldn't he?"

Elhanan squirmed, not wanting to tell his friend how ridiculous his words were. After all, Amplias was only a pagan. Rather than insult his friend, he abruptly swung the conversation in another direction. "Speculations about the future are useless, Amplias. I need more practical thinking; that which applies to the present. I've determined to earn money—a large sum of money—to buy my mother a gift. Have those ever-listening ears of yours heard of any work opportunities for someone like me?"

"Surely your father could find you employment, through knowing so many people."

"He offered to do that," Elhanan said. "But I want to do this on my own from beginning to end. That's important to me."

Amplias smiled. "Well, I've heard of one thing that might fit into your days. But I doubt the opportunity would appeal to you, or at all please your father."

"Tell me what it is. Let me decide," urged Elhanan.

"Well then, I heard of a military captain newly arrived from Rome. He's come to replace the hated Criveas. There's quite a stir because he's also replacing all the servants of the former captain. According to word here in the street, he's particularly eager to find a new stableboy. Word is that he not only values his horses but actually seems to love them, as well."

"Horses!" Elhanan breathed out the word, fired by excitement. "My mother says that all animals touch my heart, and I admit the truth of that. But . . . horses! They're so strong, so beautiful. Why, their very smell is wonderful!"

Amplias broke into Elhanan's rhapsodizing. "Caring *about* horses is, I suppose, all well and good. But could you care *for* them in the real sense?"

Elhanan jumped to his feet. "I've never had an opportunity. But I'm a quick learner, and both my mother and father say that I'm gifted with plants and creatures."

"Slow down, my friend," Amplias laughed. "You don't need to convince me. It will be the Roman captain you must persuade . . . and, of course, your father."

Elhanan was instantly sobered by mention of his father. His excitement was suddenly weighed down by the leaden certainty that Joseph would oppose anything that contributed to a Roman military man's well-being. Nevertheless he must try. First he would go to this newcomer who was seeking a stableboy. Of course a Roman of such rank might refuse even to see him. Yet if he did grant a hearing, and if he were somehow willing to consider having a Jew tend to his horses, then . . . But his thoughts mustn't race ahead so wildly. All of this might well prove to be nothing but empty dreaming. "Thank you, Amplias. You've given me the help I needed."

"I fear that, instead of help, I may have given you that which will result in disappointment and trouble. But now you must go on to your classes, eh? I feel the sun coming from a considerably higher point than when we started this conversation; you'll have to hurry."

"School? No; not today. I'll be . . . uh . . . *detained* from classes today. I have to find this Roman newcomer. But wait. His name? Do you know it, Amplias?"

Amplias nodded, closing his unseeing eyes as if to open them upon some internal list. "I've heard it spoken. Yes . . . his name is Melzar."

"Melzar," Elhanan repeated, making effort to secure the name in his memory. "I'll go at once to find him. Again, my thanks for your help." So saying, Elhanan hurried away. But he had only gone halfway along the first block before he stopped, halted by the realization of the enormous thing he was about to do. He drew a long, deep breath, then continued determinedly toward the Fortress Antonia.

How strange it felt to seek the Roman sector of the city! The crucifixion procession witnessed just moments ago came again to his mind's eye. But he quashed his revulsion and hurried along street after street, his haste earning him occasional glares of irritation from people he passed. Then, heart pumping and breath coming in short bursts, he again halted, this time feeling as if his trembling legs would give way under him. His eyes traveled upward to where the Roman fortress loomed high above. Two burly soldiers patrolled the great gateway. Elhanan straightened his tunic, ran his fingers through his hair, and fought to slow his breathing. Then he squared his shoulders and approached the less fearsome of the guards.

"Excuse me, sir." Elhanan's voice sounded embarrassingly weak to his own ears. But the soldier heard and stopped, turning to face him. He put greater force behind his next words: "I'm looking for the captain known as Melzar. Could you tell me where I might find him?"

"There are a number of places you might find him," the guard responded, not unkindly. "But what's your purpose in seeking one of our Roman commanders, Jew boy?"

Though he was stung by the term used to address him, Elhanan kept his eyes on those of his questioner. "I've heard that he needs a stableboy."

"Hmm. Hold out your hands." The order startled Elhanan, but he obeyed, stretching both hands, palms upward, toward the guard. The soldier's leather armor creaked as he bent to inspect them. "Um-hmm. Yes, your hands look more gentle than useful. Word has it that our new officer treats his mounts more like children than like horses. If that be true, perhaps you can meet his qualifications for stableboy." The guard resumed his upright stance. "All right, then. You'll find Captain Melzar in the third building—along there. Ask for him again at the doorway." As he spoke the last words, he pushed open a small walk gate.

"Thank you, sir. Thank you very much!" Elhanan scurried through the gate and moved toward the building indicated.

He repeated his request to a solemn-faced soldier who was seated inside the entrance to the third building. He suffered the guard's scornful up-and-down visual inspection, then he headed down the hallway as directed. His heart quailed at being literally surrounded by Roman soldiers. Now with every step he felt an increasing urge to turn and run out of all this strangeness, back into the familiar and safe. But he set his jaw, steeling himself against the force of his fear as he remembered the blue beads he so badly wanted to give his mother. Now, too, there was an added incentive—horses. Here in this Roman strangeness lay a chance to be near horses.

Reaching the room he sought, he stopped in the open doorway to survey the small space before him. Furnishings were sparse. A heavy table held several parchment scrolls, one of them lying open. Two chairs flanked the table. There was a map on a wall, and a metal stanchion near it, topped by a brass eagle. The room's only occupant stood looking out one of the high, barred windows. He was, as Elhanan had expected, a big man, broad across the back with arms and legs that were solidly muscled.

It was evident that the man's attention was not on the room in which he stood, and he was unaware of Elhanan's presence. That made the boy feel that he held unfair advantage by being unseen himself. So he moved his feet, deliberately scraping his sandals on the stone floor. "Captain Melzar, sir?"

The words hung unheeded in the air a moment; then the Roman turned from the window. He surveyed his young visitor silently before speaking. "Yes. I am Captain Melzar. And you are . . .?"

"Elhanan, sir."

"And what can I do for you, Elhanan?"

The boy wet his dry lips. "I heard . . . I understand . . . A friend tells me you're in need of a stableboy."

Melzar stepped to the front of the table and leaned against its edge. "Your friend told you correctly. I presume you are offering your services?"

"Y-y-yes, sir. I would very much like to be a stableboy, sir."

"Wanting the task is a good start, Elhanan. But are you suited to it? Come closer so I can get a good look at you."

Elhanan obediently moved forward, coming to within a cubit's length of the Roman. He saw a number of graying hairs at Melzar's temple and warm, sand-colored eyes.

"Tell me now exactly why you offer to be my stableboy."

"Because I admire . . . I would like to be near . . . Uh . . . Horses . . . they . . . I . . ." Elhanan stopped, mortified by his inability to express himself. He dropped his head, sick at heart in the surety that he had destroyed all chance of being hired.

Melzar took Elhanan's chin in his great hand, lifting the boy's head until their eyes met again. "I believe I understand what it is you're trying to say. Have you ever actually taken care of horses?"

"No, sir," Elhanan confessed miserably. "I've only seen horses, and watched them, and wished to be near them. They're such beautiful creatures! Their movements . . . the sounds of their hooves . . ."

Melzar's hand moved from Elhanan's chin to his shoulder. The touch was companionable. "That wish, that feeling, is love for horses, lad. There is no finer qualification for stable work. As for the work itself, however, it's not easy. Stalls must be cleaned daily; hay and oats fed; water carried; the horses themselves have to be bathed and brushed. Do you think you could manage all of that?"

His eyes shining, Elhanan breathed out his reply, "Oh, yes, sir. I'm sure I could!"

"There is yet another thing, Elhanan. Can you be depended upon? I'll not allow my mounts to be neglected—ever. In fact, that's the reason I'm now looking for a stableboy. The young fellow holding that position as a leftover from the former captain proved to be undependable. Do I make myself clear?"

"Indeed, sir. I'll do my very best, sir. My father has always taught me . . ." Crimson flooded into Elhanan's face as he mentioned his father. The little room was suddenly silent. The Roman straightened up from his leaning position and moved around to the back of his table. He sat down and carefully straightened several items on the surface of the table. When he looked up at Elhanan he had a small, knowing smile on his lips. "I judge that your father isn't aware you've come here. Am I correct?"

Elhanan hung his head. "No, sir . . . I mean yes, sir, you're right. He knows I'm looking for work, but . . . well, I doubt that he . . . that he would approve of this." Elhanan traced the outline of a floor stone with the toe of his sandal. He bit his lip, fearing an outburst of anger from this man whose time he had wasted, this powerful Roman whom he may have offended.

"It's important that all parties in an employment situation be agreed. You may tell your father that I feel you could be trained to make a fine stableboy, and that I myself would instruct you in the task."

Elhanan nodded slowly, eyes still lowered, realizing how little those things would mean in trying to persuade Joseph. As if reading his thoughts, Melzar continued.

"Tell your father, too, that Quintius Melzar, though Roman, neither scorns nor hates you Jews. And tell him, finally, that I am a father myself. I have two sons—twins—somewhat younger than you." Elhanan looked up from the floor as he felt the renewal of hope in his heart. Melzar nodded approvingly as he saw the effect of his words. "Go now. We have things to do, both you and I. I must tackle these military matters." He waved his hand toward the scrolls. "And you face a bit of battle yourself, eh? Come back, shall we say in three days? That will give your father ample time to make his decision."

The remainder of the day dragged for Elhanan. Once out of the Fortress Antonia, he wandered through Jerusalem. He told himself repeatedly that this luxury of freedom from school was wonderful. But the free time and the activities around him in the streets failed to hold his interest. All he could think about was the evening ahead and the upcoming confrontation with his father. He kept careful track of the passing hours, carefully calculating when to start his homeward journey in order to make everything appear normal. And in his later wanderings he came again to Laban's small sales table on the street near home.

"Well, well, well, Joseph's boy. You seem happier today. The way to manhood runs more smoothly somehow, eh?"

"A bit easier, Laban. I've found a place to work. Uh . . . I should say *perhaps* I've found one. If it comes to be, soon I may be able to pay for the blue beads you hold for me."

"Soon, eh?" Laban's eyes squinted more tightly. "I told you I'd not press you for payment. Nevertheless I would urge you to make that *soon* come true, Joseph's boy. Yes, yes, yes. Things may change. Unexpected things. I hear talk these days of a man called Jesus. It's interesting talk, boy. Talk about strange things. Talk about miracles. Talk about healings. Heh, heh, heh. Think now, think now, Joseph's boy. If old Laban could get these mismatched legs made even, don't think he'll come back to sit here in the street selling trinkets! No, no, no! Laban—and the special blue beads—will be gone. Gone, Joseph's boy! So, so, so."

Elhanan struck a knowing pose. "You don't make me fearful, Old One. In all these years here on the street you've heard tales of many who claimed to work miracles. My father counts them off on his fingers. Should you go to this newest supposed miracle worker, you'll only come back here to your table again, legs unchanged!"

"One never knows, boy, one never knows for sure. So just keep the possibility in mind, eh? Possibility that would mean losing the beads—beautiful blue, blue beads!"

Elhanan hurried off without answering. He left behind him all thought of Laban's blue beads. Rather, his mind was filled with horses—Melzar's horses. If only, somehow, he could persuade his father to let him accept this wonderful opportunity to work with horses!

"El*hay*nan! El*hay*nan! Happy time; we meet again, El*hay*nan!"

Elhanan felt heartsick. In his excitement at the prospect of becoming Melzar's stableboy, he had forgotten Maachah's probable lying in wait.

"What ho, El*hay*nan? You seem to have your head in clouds of dreams. Silly, womanish dreams, no doubt."

Elhanan ignored the badgering, pretending unconcern as Maachah fell into step beside him. Suddenly the bigger boy grabbed Elhanan's right arm; forced him to stop. "You mustn't hurry so, El*hay*nan! We need to talk, you and I. Talk about your name."

Elhanan groaned inwardly. This was a favorite subject with Maachah, the younger boy's name. Just as he made its pronunciation a mockery, he also made its meaning an insult.

"You must ask your father why he ever chose your name, El*hay*nan. The noble name of King David's valiant captain hangs sadly on a weak scrap like you! El*hay*nan! Where is the courage and strength that should be—?" Maachah's taunt stopped abruptly as Simeon, his father, came out of the house.

"Maachah, why are you here in the street, boy?"

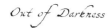

Maachah instantly released Elhanan's arm, transforming his scowl to an ingratiating smile as he turned to his father. "I was . . . visiting . . . briefly . . .with my friend Elhanan, sir."

"I'm glad you and Joseph's son are friends, Maachah. It's fitting that the sons of Council members enjoy one another's company. But your mother is looking for you. She wants to send you on some errand."

"Certainly, Father." As he moved toward his house, Maachah called over his shoulder, "Perhaps we'll have longer to visit tomorrow, *Elhaynan!*"

Watching Maachah walk quickly away, Elhanan felt both relief at the bully's departure and disgust at his two-facedness. How could a man of Simeon's rank in the Sanhedrin be so fooled by his own son? He exchanged nods with Councilor Simeon, then moved on toward home pondering the question. Maachah's father was considerably older than his own. In fact, he had served as Joseph's mentor in the Sanhedrin, acquainting him with the intricacies of its operation. His hair and brows were silver, his face wrinkled. Perhaps that was in itself part of the reason he was deceived about Maachah's character, Elhanan thought. Simeon's advanced years might form a gulf between him and his young son. Those thoughts brought Elhanan renewed gratitude for his own home. Joseph was strict as a father, but he was also loving. He spent a great deal of time talking to and listening to his son. And in times of discipline he took Elhanan's age into account in terms of behavior, character, and understanding, because he remembered his own boyhood. Simeon, by contrast, seemed more Maachah's grandfather than his father—with his parenting distanced and impaired by his years.

The first part of the evening at home passed slowly. Outside in the garden Elhanan was weighed down by the prospect of the interview with his father. He planned and then decided against many different ways to state his request. Inside the house the time spent at his mother's bedside was also difficult as he carefully avoided lying. Though he could tell Rachel nothing of the missed day of school, he held her attention by describing various characters and events seen in the streets. He included the experience of viewing the five prisoners headed for crucifixion. It helped him to put his heartsick reaction into words and to have his mother's silent, understanding squeeze of his hand. Too, as he created that word picture of Roman tyranny, Elhanan inwardly marveled at the contrast between what he sensed in the street and what he had experienced in Captain Melzar's room. Would he be able to convey that enormous difference to his father when he broached the subject of stable work for the Roman?

At last—and yet too soon—Joseph and Elhanan were alone in the garden. Rachel had been taken into the house and entrusted to Leah's bedtime care. Tobias puttered about indoors as well, getting the house itself settled for the night. Joseph sat silent in his usual place on the carved stone bench. His eyes were fixed, unseeing, upon the gathering darkness. Elhanan's throat went dry, and his palms grew sweaty. But he must speak! To delay longer was to fail through cowardly silence. Oddly, in his mind he heard Maachah's mocking—"womanly and weak El*hay*nan!" That imagined voice spurred him to speak.

"Father?"

"Yes, my son? What is it?"

"I have something to ask you." The boy sensed the effort Joseph exerted to draw his mind back from its silent, sad wanderings. Elhanan rubbed his sweaty palms on his tunic. "I've found possible work, Father. Work to earn the money needed for Mama's gift."

"So soon? Well, I see by that you're determined to acquire the necklace. What and where is this proposed work, Elhanan?"

Elhanan gulped, and his stomach knotted as if he were about to leap from a height. "You know how I love animals, Father. This is an opportunity to work with animals."

"With animals? How so?"

"Yes, sir. There is opportunity to work as a stableboy. I would go each evening to clean stalls, and to feed, and to groom."

Joseph's face showed his puzzlement. "Who offers the position, and where is the stable you would serve?"

Elhanan's fearful heartbeat was so strong it made his voice unsteady as he replied, "A kind man, Father. His name is Melzar. He's newly arrived in Jerusalem. The stable is in . . . in the Fortress. He talked with me, and—"

"The Fortress? This Melzar is a *Roman*? Is that it?"

"Yes, sir. A centurion. But, Father, he's not at all like . . . not what one would think. There's none of the Roman tyrant in him! He speaks of his horses as if they were children. He would train me himself to care for them. Oh, and he does have children too, and—"

"You cannot be serious, Elhanan! Work for a Roman? A conqueror—a tormentor of our people Israel? You would *help* such a one?"

"No, I . . . yes, but . . . I would more help his *creatures*, Father; his horses. I love horses above all other animals. I long to learn of them. Horses know no nationality, Father. Caring for them would be—"

"Enough. You've stated your case." Joseph rose from the bench and walked deeper into the garden. Elhanan saw in his father's rigidly held shoulders little sign of any favorable thoughts. But he waited silently, scarcely daring to breathe. Then Joseph slowly returned. "My first reaction is to forbid this whole thing outright. But I'll talk the matter over with your mother."

"If you could meet the captain . . . If you could only see . . ."

Joseph held up a silencing hand. "That is the end of it for tonight." Joseph turned away and moved quickly toward the house.

Elhanan, left alone in the darkening garden, shivered with the chill certainty that his request—his heart's great, double-pronged desire—would come to nought.

Chapter Four

*H*orses. Elhanan dreamed of them that night. And the next night. All night, each night. They were not easy dreams. The horses were enormous, and he had to cling desperately to their backs as they charged through battles where swords clanked upon armor, or raced through woodlands, barely missing strange, twisted trees on either side, or leaped from mountaintops and vaulted great fluffy clouds in a sunset sky. He woke before dawn after each of those night horrors feeling exhausted in both body and mind.

On the second morning, his father did not join him for the breaking of their fast. Elhanan could hear Joseph's voice, and Rachel's, coming from her room, though he couldn't distinguish their words. His stomach churned at sight of the food Leah placed before him. As he sat bound in anxious misery that would not let him eat, Leah halted her morning chores. She eased her bulk down onto a stool beside Elhanan, squinting at him in concern.

"Food seems loath to enter your mouth this morning, Elhanan. Are you unwell?"

"No, Aunt Leah. I'm fine."

"Fine!" Leah snorted the word. "When you're fine you break the night's fast with gusto, making food disappear as quickly as it's set before you. But for two mornings now you've pecked at your food as might a sick bird."

"Well, I . . ." Elhanan's weary mind balked against creating a believable response.

Leah picked up his words, attempting to lighten the boy's obvious and uncharacteristic gloom. "Well, you'll churn that goats milk to butter if you keep twirling the cup so."

Made aware of his unconscious action, Elhanan dropped his hands into his lap. Leah rose quickly. "It's honey that's needed here, I can see. A good serving of honey will—"

"No, please, Aunt Leah. I really want nothing. Nothing at all."

Joseph entered the room at that moment. "Did I hear something about Elhanan's not eating, Leah?" He crossed to the table and began piling fruit on his son's plate. "Surely a young man should know how necessary it is to eat well in preparation for his first day at work."

Elhanan slowly raised his eyes to his father's face. "At work? Do you mean . . .?"

"I mean, boy, that there are horses in a certain part of our city that will require their caretaker's strength and stamina."

"But Father, I thought . . . I never . . . I don't want you to . . ."

Joseph tousled Elhanan's hair. "You've been patient in waiting for my answer, Elhanan. I've used the time to make careful inquiries and to discuss the matter both within these walls and outside them."

Leah sniffed loudly in feigned reproach. "The master has in fact, Elhanan, fairly run the legs off my poor Tobias these two days. Such nosing about abroad and such whisperings here!"

"She's right," Joseph laughed. "But Tobias has done valuable service through his investigations. Roman he certainly is, but

Quintius Melzar is also reputed for his humanity and wisdom. His appointment to Jerusalem has already eased military hostilities toward our people. In making my decision, several considerations come into positive alignment: the facts I've learned concerning the man himself, the opportunity he offers of work with the horses, and a particular expensive purchase you have in mind."

"I may do it? I may really accept the centurion's offer?" In the overwhelming surprise, Elhanan feared the moment to be unreal—a daylight dream like those he'd known in the night, a scene conjured by his own heart's yearning.

"Yes, I'm granting the permission you asked. As you pointed out, your direct service will be to those having no nationality—horses needing good care. Your mother and I feel that besides being a stableboy, you may also play a secondary role, that of interpreter."

"Interpreter?" Elhanan echoed, puzzled.

"Indeed. It's difficult to hate people one really knows. There are of course great differences between Jews and Romans. Although we must not allow compromise between our worship of Jehovah and the Romans' worship of idols, our diverse cultures can be interpreted the one to the other. In coming to know you, Quintius Melzar may be encouraged to think more kindly of your people as a whole."

There was a brief silence as Elhanan considered his father's words.

Then a rising tide of elation swept away his sober thoughts. He jumped up from his stool, and the sudden movement sent it clattering to the floor. He flung himself into his father's arms. "Thank you, Father," he breathed. "Oh thank you, thank you!"

That day in synagogue school found Elhanan filled with constant struggle between catapulting emotion and willful determination. He ached for the school day's end so he could begin his work as Melzar's stableboy. But, too, he was convinced that his responsibility in studies must increase in gratitude for the privilege being added to his life. So each time his mind headed too strongly

toward the Fortress Antonia, he captured and redirected it, steeling himself for the study task at hand. He chuckled when not one but three of his instructors commended his close attention.

At last the rabbi's scrolls were closed and bound and the parchments carefully stored. Elhanan raced from the building. For several blocks he ran a dodging course through the city's crowds, then he slowed to a rapid walk. He didn't want to dash breathlessly into his new employer's presence. Purpose and reliability. Those must mark his service for the Roman captain. Once he arrived at the Fortress, the guards at the entrances leading to Melzar's office nodded at each other in amusement as they heard him speak gravely of his appointment with their commander.

Melzar appeared genuinely pleased by Elhanan's announcement of his father's positive decision. But he wasted no time idling. He spoke briefly to a subordinate, explaining his need to acquaint Elhanan with his new duties; then captain and stableboy left the small office together.

Elhanan thought his heart would burst as he entered the shadowing overhang that fronted the stable. The line of stalls seemed endless, and horses' heads turned toward them over the doors. The sight of great eyes and questing ears, the mingled smells of horses, leather, hay, and droppings, the sounds of nickering, snorting, and stomping, exhilarated him in a way he'd never known before. He was only able to quell threatened giddiness by repeating severely in his mind, "Purpose . . . reliability; purpose . . . reliability." Nevertheless, Melzar smiled; the boy's delight was unmistakable. That deep, instinctive love for horses was the prime requirement in the one who would care for his prized mounts.

Melzar halted halfway down the row of stalls. No heads protruded from the doors before which man and boy stood, but from inside came the low sounds of teeth munching and tails switching. Without raising his voice, Melzar spoke. "Ho, Flamma. And you, Lux." Low nickers sounded in answer, and two heads soon appeared.

Elhanan gasped. "Beautiful! They're so very beautiful."

The centurion smiled broadly. "I think they are that, of course. But it pleases me to see you're favorably impressed. No doubt you can guess which name belongs to each."

Elhanan nodded. The distinction could not have been more obvious. Flamma was accurately named, for he had a coat the color of burnished copper, a golden mane, and an irregular white blaze running the length of his great, bold face. Lux's coat was white, in keeping with his name meaning "light." His mane and tail were gray, and he had a delicate face with dappling around nostrils and mouth.

As Melzar stepped forward, both horses reached to nuzzle him. He stroked their faces gently, speaking as if to friends. "Now, my beauties, I've brought you someone who will care for you more consistently than I." Turning to Elhanan, he continued, "Here, young man. Come greet your charges."

Feeling as if he walked through water, Elhanan moved forward, reached out, and felt the soft muzzles touch his open hands. As he stroked their cheeks, the horses nosed his chest, blowing softly. His heart experienced the warmth of delight.

"Good. It's evident you like one another. So now let's go on to explain your duties." The Roman concisely set forth what he wanted for the horses' daily care, explaining and demonstrating the tasks. Then he watched Elhanan perform each assignment. Giving the horses a final pat, Melzar finished his instructions by saying, "There's no meanness in either of these fellows, Elhanan, but a carelessly placed hoof can crush your foot, or a startled kick break your leg. Be watchful, and always let a horse know, by voice and by touch, exactly where you are. Now, if you've no questions, I must leave and let you set to work."

"Yes, sir. I mean no, sir, I've no questions. I promise to work well, sir. I'll do my very best."

"After these past moments together here, I'm confident of that. And for good work you'll receive fair wages. Will payment once a fortnight be agreeable?"

Elhanan was surprised by the mention of payment. He had been so absorbed with the horses and Melzar's instructions that he had momentarily forgotten his practical motive for working: purchasing the blue beads for his mother. But he collected his wits enough to say, "Whatever suits you will be fine with me, sir."

The Roman moved away several steps then turned back with a final thought. "I doubt it will be long before your work is interrupted by two small whirlwinds spouting every sort of question and suggestion. Those will be my twin sons, Nicanor and Vicanor. Their seven years of life have added much noise and many pranks to our household. They love to come to the stables, but if their antics bother you, or you find their presence distracting, don't hesitate to send them home to their mother."

Melzar left the stable area, and Elhanan entered the cubicle that contained harness and equipment. Attaching a leather bucket to each end of a short wooden yoke, he hoisted the unit to his shoulders and moved out into the courtyard toward the fountain from which Fortress animals were watered. He set the buckets with their yoke on the ground, took the large clay dipper from its iron hook, and began filling the buckets.

The minutes flew as Elhanan concentrated on watering and feeding the horses and cleaning their stalls. Rather than tiring from the work, his energies increased. He could barely contain his excitement as he approached the final task of grooming his charges. He went to the equipment cubicle for the cloths and brushes Melzar had shown him. In his haste he dropped one of the cloths, and as he bent to retrieve it the back of his neck prickled with the sense of someone's presence. He turned quickly, and found two small boys standing shoulder to shoulder in the doorway, their eyes solemnly fixed upon him. *Twin sons*, Melzar had said, but the term had left Elhanan unprepared for the human mirror images now standing before him. He looked from one to the other, searching in vain for some distinguishing mark. It was evident that his puzzlement amused the twins. Both grinned.

"Our father didn't tell you we're twins?" The question came from the boy on the right.

"He told me, yes, but he didn't say how wholly alike you are. Is there some way to distinguish between you?" Elhanan smiled wryly, still trying to detect some helpful differentiation.

Now the twin on the left spoke. "Our names, of course, are different. I'm Nicanor."

"And I'm Vicanor," chimed the other.

"But other than having you announce your identity, as now, how may I know which name applies to which?" Elhanan held out his hands in helpless appeal.

"Our family and a few close friends can tell us apart," began Nicanor.

"But there *is* one small mark which separates us. We show it to those we feel will be our friends," continued Vicanor.

"Ah, I understand." said Elhanan. "And will I have such trust?"

The twins kept their gaze fixed upon Elhanan. "We're not sure," Vicanor answered slowly.

Nicanor, in the thought-completing manner Elhanan would find to be habitual in the twins, went on, "We've never known a Jew before. Not really."

"We see some merchants now and then, but you're a boy," Vicanor said hesitantly.

Nicanor took up the thought. "And you'll be here . . . helping . . . by taking care of Lux and Flamma daily. So . . ."

"So," Elhanan responded, "I hope we can be friends. It will require learning on both our parts. Because, you see, except for a beggar boy named Amplias, I've never known Romans before either."

"Oh!" The twins spoke in unison.

"In fact, I've never known twins—whether Roman or Jew. So my learning must be even greater than yours. Shall we work at the lessons together?"

The boys nodded their agreement. Then Vicanor stepped toward Elhanan, turned his head to the side, and pulled his left ear slightly forward.

Nicanor spoke from the doorway. "See? There's the mark that separates us. Vicanor has a mole behind his left ear."

Elhanan nodded. "Ah, I see. Thank you. I may have to rely on the mole for some time before I know you well enough to tell you apart! Now—would you like to help me with the horses?"

Vicanor, returning to his brother's side, answered. "Father won't let us go into the stalls unless he's with us."

"He says we must wait until we're older," Nicanor went on.

"And larger," Vicanor completed.

Elhanan chuckled, thinking that it would take time not only to distinguish between the twins, but to grow accustomed to having one thought spoken by two mouths, as well. To the boys he said, "Your father is very wise. He warned me, too, of the hurts that can happen quickly with horses. Shall we agree, then, that I'll work inside, and you two outside the stall?"

"Yes!" The twins again spoke, now in eager unison.

So began the arrangement that was to become routine to the three boys. The twins hung side by side on the door of whichever stall Elhanan occupied at the moment. They watched his every move, commenting, suggesting, or simply chattering. Elhanan tried to make them feel useful by letting them hold or fetch various items and hand them to him as needed. He wasn't bothered by the twins' watchful presence. His delighted focus was on the animals he tended—the warmth and aroma of their firm flesh, the glistening silk of their coats, their ears flicking toward him as he moved from place to place, and the gentle blowing of their nostrils as they occasionally nuzzled him on shoulder, leg, hand, or face.

He finished grooming the horses, straightened and closed the equipment cubicle, and bade the twins goodbye. As the younger boys scurried away, Elhanan realized with a jolt that for the first time in many months his mind had been free of sorrowful concern for his mother. Later, as he and his father sat together in the garden's late-evening darkness, he mentioned the freedom from thoughts of Rachel he'd experienced and his feeling of guilt because of it.

Joseph, leaning forward with elbows on his knees, slowly moved the toe of one sandaled foot back and forth on the soft earth. He paused briefly before responding to Elhanan's confession. "Don't be burdened with guilt, Son. Rather, we should thank Jehovah for this distraction He has made possible through your work with the horses. Both you and I are failing to obey the Book of the Law by carrying the burden of your mother's illness so much on our own hearts. The Psalmist would remind us to cast that burden—and every burden, however heavy it may be—upon the Lord Jehovah." Joseph straightened from his bent position and turned toward Elhanan. "This talk of burdens reminds me that in my concern for your mother I've also failed to advance your spiritual training as I should have. That failure, too, points back to weakness in my faith and Scripture obedience, and it must displease Jehovah. Beginning at this moment, we must together increase our efforts both in prayer for your mother and in preparing you for manhood. As an important part of that latter project, I believe it's time for you to witness sacrifices in the temple."

That night Elhanan's dreams were vivid and frightening. He again rode mighty steeds, but in each dream he and his mount were fleeing some awful threat. Despite their frantic efforts to escape, they were caught, and the horse was snatched from under him. Then hulking, faceless men threw the animal to its side and bound its legs. Twice he woke with pounding heart because the dark dream figures were advancing upon the helpless horse with great knives in their raised hands.

Elhanan spent the remainder of the week alternating between the wish that time would fly so he could be with the horses, and the dread of its flight because each day also brought him closer to the temple sacrifice he was to witness.

When the evening before the chosen day came, Elhanan struggled against his ever-lower spirits. He wondered why he felt such dread and downheartedness. His father's promise to take him to the temple sacrifices marked a step forward in his transition to maturity. Why then was he filled with reluctance? His self-questioning kept him unusually quiet through the evening meal and later in the garden. After a considerable length of time spent sitting silently together, Joseph spoke, his voice gentle. "Elhanan, it's not wrong or weak to feel as you do. Your mother and I have sensed your struggle these past days. It calls to mind my own feelings long ago when I first faced attending temple sacrifices."

Elhanan was startled. "You, Father? But I thought . . ."

"If the truth were known, my son, there are few who can view the sacrifices without regretful feelings. Surely that heart response serves a part in Jehovah's purpose. Our pity when we see animals killed reminds us of our sin's seriousness. Although in His mercy Jehovah recognizes the weakness of our human flesh and its sinful tendencies, in His justice He demands the death penalty for sin. And the demand is met when an animal dies in substitution."

Elhanan felt his thinking cleared and his heart comforted by his father's words, and he soon retired to his small room. There he prepared for bed. Following his prayers, he fell into deep, dreamless sleep.

Caring for Captain Melzar's horses became more and more a time and place of refuge for Elhanan. The physical work offset the tension of his heightened studies in school and at home, and the twins' chattering presence lightened his thinking during the stable hours.

Beyond the time he spent caring for the horses, Elhanan felt new motivation to delve into the Torah for himself. He had been shaken by Amplias' suggestion that the Messiah might be unlikely in his kingship. Surely that couldn't be true. His people's glorious rescuer and restorer must come mounted on a splendid steed, a great horse more beautiful and strong than any now in the Roman stables! And yet he wondered.

Joseph, too, had intensified his Torah studies for his own sake as well as for teaching Elhanan. The problems and possibilities of the Messiah's coming became an increasingly common topic of discussion between father and son in the cool evenings.

All of life seemed to be taking on a more serious bent for Elhanan. It happened rather suddenly—the change in some indefinable way connected to the temple sacrifices to which Joseph had introduced his son.

Elhanan's first visit to the temple was forever burned into his mind. All of his senses had been tuned to the highest pitch of awareness. Each time the memory returned he experienced again not just the sights but the smells and sounds of the experience as well.

Joseph and Elhanan had joined throngs of people crowding the outer Court of the Women. Many of them were worshippers, others moneychangers and sellers of sacrificial animals. Joseph quickly selected and paid for a dun-colored bull calf. The boy's heart ached as he prodded the reluctant little animal from behind and Joseph pulled from ahead toward one of the priests' stations. There the calf was killed, skinned, dissected, and washed. Then, accompanied by the priest, father and son moved on into the inner court, the Court of Israel. There smaller, more intense groups of men milled about or moved in one of the several lines approaching the great altar. When their time came, Joseph and Elhanan helped the priest lift their sacrifice onto the great stone altar; watched as the blood was sprinkled in the prescribed manner; prayed for their sins' forgiveness, for their genuine consecration, and for Rachel's healing as the smoke ascended from the burning meat.

Elhanan sensed that life would not—could not—ever be the same after that day. At the instant of the calf's slaughter, sin became real and personal. Although his father had explained Jehovah's principle of blood sacrifice, the reality was profoundly moving. How truly awful was sin! He determined to strive harder to keep the Law of God.

Elhanan shook himself, determined to be rid of the temple memory for the moment. The mental pictures, unbidden, had filled his mind while he combed Lux's tail. He was glad that for once Vicanor and Nicanor had failed to appear, for they would have noticed his distraction. He patted the horse. "Sorry, my friend. Did you fear I'd comb this lovely tail right off of you?"

"Elhanan! Ho, is my stableman about?"

Elhanan quickly exited the stall. "Here, sir." Standing before the door, he felt Lux's head come over his shoulder to look, as he himself was doing, toward Melzar's approach. Flamma's head appeared in the doorway of the next stall, and he nickered toward his master.

"Ah yes. There you are, surrounded, I see, by your charges. How are you getting on with these two great babies?" Melzar stopped between the two stall doors, a hand reaching out to caress each of the horses.

"Fine, sir. I hope their care has been acceptable."

Melzar laughed. "More than acceptable, my young friend. Since you took up your duties here, these two are growing as sleek, as fat, as contented, as the stable's tabby cat there, who owes her own fine health to an endless supply of mice."

"I'm glad, sir. Is there anything more—or different—you'd have me do?"

The captain sighed. "I do need to ask you to do a bit more than what we first agreed upon. There is far more paperwork demanding my attention here than I had expected. Much to my regret, none of that can be done on horseback. And my men have their own mounts' care upon them, besides their assigned duties both here in the Fortress and abroad. What would you say, then, to my request that you add riding to your duties of grooming and feeding?"

"Riding?" Elhanan's single word was a mixture of gasp and exclamation.

"Ah, I gather that wouldn't displease you. Good. It's clear that you have an aptitude with horses. Your effectiveness on the floor of the stable bodes well for the same once you're mounted. I've found that neither age nor training is essential in handling horses, but rather the kind of instinct you show. Too, the exercise grounds are confined and well within view, providing scant chance of the animals' serious misbehavior or your injury. It simply comes down to this: If these two beasts continue to stand about in their stalls for days on end, they'll grow so lazy they'll be unfit for the Roman Imperial Army! Exercise is the need. And since parchment makes me its prisoner these days, horse exercising must be done by another." As he spoke, Melzar had taken a bridle from its hook in the adjacent cubicle. "Come with me here, into Flamma's stall." The horse obligingly moved aside as the two entered. Going to Flamma's head, Melzar described and demonstrated for the boy how the bridle was to be put on. Then he led the great red horse outside and handed the reins to Elhanan. "Now if you will move this, our bigger fellow, out into the courtyard, I'll put a headstall on Lux too."

Elhanan watched the whole bridling and saddling process with great concentration, yet as if in a happy dream. Melzar then showed the boy how to mount, explaining, "We'll start you today on Lux. Though both horses are gentle and finely trained, Flamma's greater size might be a bit intimidating at the start. I see by the sundial we've an hour yet before you must leave. So, follow me." Melzar swung up onto Flamma's back. With Elhanan following on Lux, they crossed the stable courtyard to an archway Elhanan had noticed but never entered. He was surprised to find it a passageway crossing under one wing of the fortress. Once through its shadowed, echoing length, they came to a great iron-studded gate. Roman sentries were posted to either side. The sentries snapped to attention at sight of their commander. Melzar drew Flamma to a halt and spoke to the sentries.

"How goes the watch?"

"No disturbance to report, sir," the larger of the two replied. "Only our own men going in and out. Each is duly noted."

"Excellent. This . . ." he turned to indicate Elhanan, "is my stableman. He's proving so fine with my mounts' earthbound care that I'm promoting him to some that is more, shall we say, lofty."

The sentries smiled, their tension easing in response to the commander's light spirit.

"On certain days hereafter, Elhanan will be coming through the gate to take the horses out onto the exercise grounds. While he puts his mounts through their paces, I want you to watch, making certain that nothing untoward occurs. Note these instructions both for yourselves and for any others who draw this watch. The exercising will last for approximately one hour. Then be ready for Elhanan to bring the horses in through the gate again."

"Of course, sir. We understand." The sentries saluted, then they moved together to unlock and swing open one half of the great gate.

Passing through the gate, Elhanan saw a large enclosed field with hoof-pocked trails running its length and breadth. Here and there were obstacles across the trails, some of stone, others of logs. Melzar pulled Flamma to a stop. Sweeping his hand toward the field, he said, "Twice around the course for each horse and once over the jumps each day will keep my beauties in shape. So let's begin."

If this be dreaming, may I never wake, thought Elhanan. It was not dreaming, but rather exciting, glorious reality. Melzar was clear in his instructions. He taught what to do with hands, legs, and torso through all the horses' varied paces, as well as in the low jumps. His demonstrated riding skills were superb. Elhanan silently vowed that, given the chance, he too would become such a horseman.

After several rounds of the field, Melzar rode close to Elhanan. He smiled, leaning to pat the boy on the shoulder. "It's as I thought. You have natural talent for horses. You sit firmly, and your hands are sensitive. You'll do well with both my mounts. In fact, let's trade horses now. You need to sense the differences between the two."

With Elhanan now on Flamma and Melzar on Lux, they set off again around the exercise field. Elhanan concentrated, seeking to learn the characteristics that set the horses apart under saddle. Both responded quickly to rein and leg; each frequently flicked his ears back as if listening for spoken commands from the rider. The real difference, Elhanan decided, was a matter of personality. Lux was smooth and steady, like the breeze that visited the garden at home each morning. Flamma, on the other hand, was a bundle of latent energy and strength.

As they drew abreast again, Melzar laughed. "You seem more serious when mounted on Flamma. Does he trouble you in some way?"

"No, sir. I only meant to understand his heart, and how to respond to it."

"Good! And what would you say of those differences? Which horse do you favor?"

Elhanan frowned. "Favor? I don't favor either. Each is . . . himself."

"That's a well-spoken judgment. Then let me ask this. Which would you choose for a long-distance gallop carrying an urgent message?"

After thinking a moment, Elhanan replied, "That would be Flamma."

"And for battle? Which?"

"Lux." Elhanan was immediate with this response.

Melzar nodded. "Most interesting. Just opposite from what a casual observer would say. Ah, one more thing before we return to the stables. Here is a hitch post. When you bring both horses, you can tether one here while exercising the other."

The return trip to the stable was silent except for the sounds of the horses' hooves and the creaking of leather. But the silence was comfortable rather than awkward.

As they dismounted, Melzar spoke again. "So. Do you think you can add this greater duty to your list?"

"Oh yes, and gladly, sir. Thank you for giving me the opportunity."

"You've proven trustworthy within the stables and stable yard, and today you've proven that you have a natural aptitude, all indicating you're capable of added responsibility. Ah yes—and this you've earned, as well—your first fortnight's pay." The captain handed him a small leather bag of coins.

Elhanan's feet flew over the cobblestones as he made his way home. His hands held, literally, multiple reasons for boundless joy—the lingering scent of horseflesh and saddle leather, and the purse containing the first payment toward his mother's necklace.

He raced to the corner where Amplias sat begging. Breathless, he plopped down beside his friend. "Amplias, can you spare a moment?"

The beggar turned his sightless eyes toward his Jewish friend. "Of course. Your ragged breathing tells me you've not sauntered through the streets today. So my moment spared can allow you a moment's rest."

Elhanan shook his head. "Rest? I don't need rest today! I could run on all the way home. Captain Melzar has asked me to *ride* Lux and Flamma! Can you imagine that?"

Amplias frowned. "Wouldn't you prefer a donkey, Elhanan? My ears tell me that horses are very large . . . and strong."

"They are, indeed. But as to your question, no—a hundred times no—I'd not prefer a donkey! Oh, I wish I could tell you the joy of riding, Amplias. I wish you could know."

Amplias' smile broke the dusky surface of his face. "I'm content to experience it here," he tapped his temple. "So tell me of it."

Elhanan related the afternoon's happenings, describing for his blind friend the emotions he had known as well as the physical details of the experience. "And then Captain Melzar gave me wages for this past fortnight's work!" Elhanan drew the small leather bag with its precious contents from under his sash. "Here, Amplias.

Isn't it amazing? *Wages* for hours of joy! Payment to go toward my mother's gift."

Amplias took the purse from Elhanan and weighed it speculatively in his hand. Then his voice took on a bantering note as he said, "A fortnight's wage in here, is it? My friend, on a good day I can accumulate this much without moving from my place right here!"

Elhanan laughed, catching the purse as Amplias tossed it back to him. "Should passersby learn the richness of your mind, they might well withhold both their sympathy and their alms."

"No. Those who can see the stones in the street can't see that blindness doesn't mean stupidity and helplessness. But enough of this banter. We both must move on to the business at hand, eh? Me to my day's collection, and you to make payment to Old Laban?"

Elhanan rose quickly. "I'm afraid payment must wait until tomorrow. The lengthening shadows urge me to hurry home. So, for now, farewell."

Making his way on through still-crowded streets, Elhanan all at once realized that he must be grinning. Unknown people were glancing his way, registering surprise, then smiling at him. Well, hadn't he reason to grin? Wasn't there, at this moment, a comforting bulge where the coin-filled leather purse rested under his sash?

"And why the silly grin today, El*hay*nan?"

Elhanan groaned inwardly as he faced the prospect of Maachah's bullying again. But today he felt less than his usual level of terror as the bigger boy moved toward him.

"Hello, Maachah. Isn't smiling allowed here?"

"Well, well. Aren't you the wise-mouth one today! But, NO! You may not smile!"

Elhanan walked on steadily toward the bully. "Then I'll frown. Will that please you better?"

"How dare you, you little—" Suddenly Elhanan stopped; not because of Maachah, but because of something else—a pitiful bleating close at hand.

Maachah's eyes glittered. "Aha. So you've heard the voice of my new pet! Alas, she seems not to care greatly for her master. Let's see what the problem is, shall we, El*hay*nan?" Maachah moved to a low growth of greenery against the wall of a nearby building. Reaching behind the bush, he lifted out a tiny black and white goat. The creature could not have been more than a fortnight from its mother's womb. But its size and infancy were not what caught Elhanan's attention. Instead it was the creature's torment. Clotted blood covered two of its tiny hooves. As Maachah lowered the goat to the ground, Elhanan saw that the bleeding feet, right front to left rear, were bound together with a short length of cord. When the kid tried to walk, only its two free legs could move normally; the two that were tied crumpled, and the cord tore cruelly into the flesh.

The struggling kid bleated pitifully, and Maachah roared with laughter. "Hilarious, isn't it! She looks more like a beetle than a goat, scooting along like that!"

Elhanan grew heartsick as he looked from the suffering animal to its delighted torturer. "Stop this, Maachah!"

The bigger boy wiped tears of laughter from his eyes. "Stop? Of course not. I've not had so much fun for days."

"Please. Free the poor creature." Elhanan's voice cracked in emotion.

"What? Begging for a goat? Such silliness becomes you, El*hay*nan." Maachah nudged the kid roughly with his foot, making it increase its struggles. The grass under the little animal reddened with its blood.

Elhanan could bear it no longer. He reached into his sash and pulled out the leather purse. "Here. I have coins, Maachah. Take it. Take it all. I'll buy the goat from you."

Maachah's laughter stopped abruptly. He looked at Elhanan through squinted eyes. "Coins? Where would one such as you acquire them? I'd wager that bag contains only stones picked up along the street. Let me see what it is you claim to be coins."

With his hands trembling, Elhanan loosened the drawstring on the leather purse and spilled Melzar's coins into his palm. "See?

Are these stones picked up along the street? Sell me the goat." Elhanan held his breath, afraid that Maachah's delight in torture might outweigh his greed. But to his relief, the bigger boy nodded in assent.

"Done. You've proven your foolishness yet again, El*hay*nan. What a waste of money! But the stupid creature is yours. You deserve each other." He reached for the coins.

Elhanan shook his head, slowly putting the coins back into their leather pouch. "I'll not take her bound like that, Maachah. Cut the cords. When she comes to me, she comes to freedom."

Elhanan was surprised by the boldness of his own words; he was more surprised when Maachah set about removing the cords. When the bloody binding fell away, Elhanan tossed the purse toward Maachah. The toss purposely forced the bully away from the goat. Elhanan darted forward and snatched the little animal as it lay panting on the ground. Then, with the kid in his arms, he moved away down the street toward home.

"A poor bargain, El*hay*nan," Maachah called after him. "You're soft in the head, El*hay*nan. But bring your gold to me any day, any day at all!" The mocking cry followed Elhanan down the street. As the voice faded, however, Elhanan's own mind took up the taunt. He looked down at the black-and-white bundle in his arms. A poor bargain indeed. In fact this creature was no bargain at all. And what was he going to do with the animal from this point on? A goat, of all things! A ridiculous, useless little she-goat for which he had given his very first fortnight's earnings! As the thoughts tumbled over one another, Elhanan's steps slowed. Not only had he made a bad bargain, he had squandered the first payment toward his mother's gift.

Elhanan looked down again at the animal he held against his chest. At that moment the kid raised its head. He had never been close to a goat before. The creature's eyes were yellow and the pupils rectangular! He couldn't suppress a smile as he examined the kid's face. And when the miniature mouth opened to produce a plaintive bleat, Elhanan laughed out loud. "So . . . at least *you* are pleased with the bargain, eh? As well you should be. There's no way to imagine the further tortures Maachah may have had in mind for you. And, bargain or not, you're now mine. We must think what's to be done with you."

Chapter Five

*L*eah and Tobias were working in the courtyard as Elhanan entered the gate. Tobias was on his knees reaching into the outdoor oven's firing chamber with a long-handled tool. Leah, stooping to watch, gave suggestions and directions. Elhanan's heart fell when he saw them. He had hoped for time alone to think things through and devise some sort of plan regarding the little goat. But it was not to be. He had barely cleared the gate when the kid gave a prolonged bleat.

Leah whirled toward the sound, and her jaw dropped when she saw Elhanan and what he held in his arms. Tobias withdrew his arms from the firing chamber, looked over his shoulder, and froze in surprise, his ash-blackened hands resting on the tool he had been using. Then both began to move and speak at once.

The two servants' words and voices competed so badly that at first Elhanan could make no sense of what they were saying.

Leah's was the first understandable sentence. "What is that creature, Elhanan, and where did you get it?"

"I . . . she . . . I bought her. It's a goat. But just a very little one—a kid."

Tobias's eyebrows climbed toward his hairline. "A goat! But such a young kid shouldn't have been taken from its dam. Why do you have it?"

The increasingly loud bleat of the goat added to the babble of overlapping questions. Elhanan had to raise his voice in order to make himself heard. "I *had* to buy her. She has no mother, and . . ."

Leah put her hands on her hips. "You were *forced* to such a thing? I know of no merchant in all of Jerusalem who demands that orphan goats be purchased."

"It wasn't a merchant, Aunt Leah. It was Maachah."

"Maachah? That overgrown young lout? It's hard to imagine his being interested in goats." Tobias's words trailed off.

Elhanan bit his lower lip to keep it from trembling. "Maachah is interested in any creature that's small, or weak, or helpless."

"Just as I thought!" snorted Leah. "I've seen the gleam of cruelty in his eyes since he was old enough to speak his own name."

"Now, Leah. Don't weave a story tapestry before Elhanan even gives us the thread of facts!" Tobias reached to restrain his wife but drew his hand back when he saw that it was still blackened with ashes.

"Hmph. However the goat came from Maachah to you, the creature's bleating will drive all of us senseless!" Leah flapped her hands at Elhanan as if shooing her next words toward him. "Put a finger in its mouth, boy. It's but a baby; sucking will quiet it."

Surprised, Elhanan experimentally offered a finger. Immediately the little mouth opened to accept it. Gentle sucking noises replaced the pathetic bleats. Elhanan chuckled as the goat's rough tongue worked vainly to coax milk from his finger. The animal's body relaxed in his arms.

Leah heaved a great sigh of relief. "Now. Tell us how it is that Maachah and this goat have conspired to bring . . . to bring disquiet to Master Joseph's courtyard!"

Elhanan carried his burden to the nearest stone bench and gratefully sat down. Then he described for the two servants how Maachah had bound and abused the kid. As he told of the goat's tortured struggles, Tobias's brows drew closer and closer together in a fierce frown until they met in an unbroken line above his nose. Leah's face reddened with anger.

"So you see, I had no choice. There was nothing to do but pay for the creature's release." Elhanan finished his tale and looked from one to the other of his two listeners for some sign of understanding.

Leah cleared her throat and made much of looking down to straighten the sash at her great waist. "That's true. You did what was right."

Tobias vehemently nodded agreement. "King Solomon said long ago that a good man is kind to a beast," he said.

Elhanan sighed, grateful for the servants' changed attitude, but still worried by the problems the goat presented. "I wish Solomon had gone on to say something about the price of kindness! As I see it, the price is high. The beast and its care are now mine."

Leah became brisk. "Well then, let's think first of food for its empty belly. Hmmm. I've a small, new oil lamp that can be put to use. With a bit of the cloth I use for straining cheese, I believe we can make a milk vessel of sorts." She bustled into the house. Tobias, meanwhile, moved back toward the oven.

"It's clear that you need some help, Elhanan. After we soothe the kid with milk, you and I can take a look at its poor cut legs. I'll use some of these ashes to make a poultice."

Elhanan sat in grateful quiet as the two servants so efficiently came to his aid. He looked down at the little goat. Its sucking had slowed to a near stop, and the yellow eyes had closed in exhausted sleep. A great warmth of tenderness and affection spread through the boy's heart, melting his cold uncertainties.

With Leah's coaching, Elhanan fed the little goat warm milk from the oil lamp, using the spout as a nipple. Then he and Tobias applied a paste of ashes to its bloody legs. They were still at the bandaging when Joseph came home. As Elhanan had expected, his father's first reaction to the goat's presence was negative. But Elhanan told the story of rescue from Maachah, with both Leah and Tobias voicing their pity for the animal and their willingness to help in its care; soon Joseph's attitude changed, and he promised to think about the matter.

At bedtime Elhanan again helped Tobias remove the bloody bandages and apply ashy paste to the kid's injuries, then they wrapped the wounds in clean scraps of cloth that Leah contributed from her sewing basket. Joseph watched, unnoticed, as the three concocted a makeshift bed, placed the animal in it, and pushed bed and goat into a corner where the house and garden walls met.

Elhanan knew that after he went to his room for the night his father would tell his mother the story of the goat. Although Rachel was gentle spirited, it was hard to imagine her taking kindly to their beautiful garden being threatened by a resident goat. But what would be the end of the helpless little creature if it was not allowed to stay? He shivered as he remembered the young animals slaughtered at the temple. The kid was so small, and helpless, and warm. But experiencing all of that could change in an instant if his parents decided the goat must go to the market or to the priests. Elhanan lay long awake, staring into the darkness, his mind in a turmoil of uncertainties.

He was both relieved and disappointed to find that Joseph had gone from home before the morning meal. "Some special, early meeting of the Council had been called, he said," Uncle Tobias reported.

Aunt Leah spoke from across the room, but she kept her back turned. "Though he had to go early, he left a message for you. He and Mistress Rachel have decided that the goat can stay. Knowing your mother, I think it was her soft heart that swayed the decision.

She actually said to me this morning that perhaps less of quiet in our garden might be a good thing! Little does she realize how quickly that animal might eat the flowers, and . . ."

Uncle Tobias moved to his wife and put a hand on her arm. "The decision has been made, Leah. We'll honor it, and make whatever adjustments of care that may be necessary . . . without complaint, eh?"

"Hmph." Leah clamped her lips tightly on the sound and hurried from the room.

For several days the goat proved to be an ideal pet. Because of the wounds suffered at Maachah's hands, she remained mostly inactive. She was satisfied to eat, sleep, and relish Elhanan's attentions.

Elhanan was glad for those peaceful days, for when he had to tell Laban that he couldn't make a payment toward the necklace's purchase, the old street vendor was sharp in his response.

"Eh, eh, eh? What kind of a story is this you tell me, boy? A goat, you say? A goat such as you see here in the streets of Jerusalem every day? And a very small goat at that? Money spent for a goat. For a *goat*! Coins you had meant to put here." Laban tapped his left palm repeatedly with his right forefinger. "That payment placed here, I remind you, would have gone toward a beautiful gift for your mother."

"I know, Laban, and I'm sorry. I didn't mean to keep the money from you. In fact, if I'd not stayed late that day exercising the horses, I would have come straight here."

"So, boy; so, so, so. You did not come straight to old Laban. Instead the fates took you another way. Another way so they could divert your payment. Divert it to the purchase of a *goat*!"

At the reference to fates, Elhanan bristled. The pagan notion of capricious gods endlessly tricking human beings revolted him. "No, Laban. There were no fates directing my steps or scorning my actions. The Torah says plainly that Jehovah God directs our steps."

The old man cackled, throwing back his head in the merriment of the moment. "Hee, hee, hee. So it was Jehovah who sent you that other way—toward a *goat*."

Ignoring the jibe, Elhanan continued earnestly. "Jehovah does direct our steps. And the Psalmist says His love is tender. I don't think it strange that His tenderness might undertake for one of His most helpless creatures."

The vendor set about straightening his wares, avoiding the boy's gaze. "Well, well, well. This argument is fruitless. The matter comes down to this: now that your coins have been squandered for an orphan goat, what am I to do with the necklace I've kept from other buyers?"

Miserable with the knowledge that he couldn't make things worse, Elhanan blurted, "Could you—please—keep the beads another fortnight? I'll be paid again at that time, and—"

"And . . . and . . . and . . . what? You'll come at last with the first of the money promised? Until then you expect old Laban to go on denying himself profit from the sale of these beads?" The wrinkled brown hands pulled the lustrous necklace from its hiding place.

Elhanan's heart sank. At sight of the beads, the full impact of what he had forfeited overwhelmed him. He shook his head. "No," he said softly, "I don't expect that. It was wrong of me to ask. You must, of course, sell the necklace. I'll find something else."

A growl rumbled from the old man's chest. "Laban the Vendor, they call me. Laban the Vendor. Ha! Laban the Foolish they must hereafter name me, for I'll keep the necklace yet another fortnight without having the earnest money. But it's only for the sake of your mother I do this thing. And you must not noise it about, or everyone in all of Jerusalem will beset Laban the Foolish, seeking goods without payment!"

Elhanan could not believe his ears. "You'll save the beads for me?"

"No, no, no. Not for you, Joseph's boy. For your dear mother. Well, stop standing there looking goose-eyed. I must get on about my business, offering my wares to those who keep their gold in their purses for things that matter! Go now. Go, go, go!"

And Elhanan went with every springing step energized by thankfulness. Surely Jehovah was good, just as his father and mother had assured him all his life. As his heart exulted over God's care, he also ached for those who, like Amplias and Laban, knew nothing of that gracious God. How bleak their existence must be! As he moved on toward synagogue school, Elhanan determined to be still more diligent in his study of the Torah, that he might better represent Jehovah.

The remainder of the day went well. However when he reached home after school and stable, he found that things had not gone well there, thanks to his little goat's improving health.

Elhanan could hear Leah's voice before he entered the courtyard gate. "I knew it. I knew it. Our household will never be the same. Look at that. Just look! How will we ever—"

Breaking into a quick trot, Elhanan interrupted Leah's wails. "What has happened? Is something wrong?"

The servant whirled to face Elhanan. "Wrong? Is something wrong, you ask? Indeed it is wrong! And it's that wretched little *goat* that's wrong! Wrong to be here."

"But what has she done?"

With her voice modulating from the earlier shrieked exclamations to incomprehensible mutterings, Leah moved to a rock near the goat's bedding corner. She pointed with a shaking hand to the rock. Following the direction of her pointing finger, Elhanan studied the shapeless multicolored something atop the stone, but failed to understand how it could put Leah into such a state.

"There. There, young master! See for yourself the trouble that creature has caused. How an animal so small could make a mess so awful, I cannot conceive."

Elhanan moved closer. As Leah's complaints continued to fill his ears, he suddenly understood. The multicolored something was—or had been—a length of bright cloth.

"This is where I dry my new-dyed fabrics for the items your mother asks me to make. But see. See! That miserable goat took my cloth to be her playground."

There was a flash of black and white as the culprit frisked into view. She bounced along on legs now healing from their cuts, her short tail held aloft like a tiny flag. She headed straight for the cloth-draped rock. Giving a single leap, she landed in the middle of the brightly colored patch. Then she began a playful little dance, scuffling the fabric so that it moved into ridges and ruffles everywhere her hooves touched. Leah and Elhanan were both speechless as they watched. Leah was just beginning to find her voice again when the creature stopped her capering, lowered her head, and began to chew the fabric. Horrified, both boy and servant yelled a protest.

"No! Get off there!" Leah flapped her skirt at the goat, but the interrupted chewing only made the goat renew her pawing dance.

"Come here, you—" and Elhanan scooped the kid from its ill-chosen play yard.

As Leah gathered up the tattered fabric amid groans and threats, Elhanan pulled brightly colored threads from the goat's mouth. "I'm sorry, Leah. I never thought . . . I didn't know that you spread fabric here, or that the goat would—"

"What is it? What's happening?" Rachel stood in the doorway, leaning against its frame. Both Leah and Elhanan were shocked to silence at seeing his mother. She looked from one to the other of them, trying to comprehend the scene before her. "I say, what is it, Leah?"

"The goat, Mistress; it's Elhanan's goat." Leah stammered.

"What of the goat?" As she spoke, Rachel moved from the doorway to sit on a nearby bench. "I take it the creature has committed some offense."

"An offense! It certainly *has* committed an offense. Just as I warned it would, the pesky thing—"

Rachel turned to Elhanan. "Since you're holding the *pesky thing*, Son, perhaps you could tell me . . ."

Elhanan licked his dry lips. "She was—playing, Mother . . . And she's only a baby, really, she didn't know . . ."

"Playing on this," Leah snatched the tattered cloth from the rock and exhibited it dramatically, "the fabric I chose so carefully yesterday in the market and spread here to dry after dyeing it. That's where the creature was playing! Rumpling and mussing it with those sharp little hooves. Nor did she stop with pawing the piece. No, she did this, as well." Leah moved to where Rachel sat, showing her the fabric's chewed places.

As the red-faced Leah pointed out bite hole after bite hole, Rachel began to laugh. Elhanan and Leah stared at her, then looked questioningly at each other. "Forgive me, you two. I can't help laughing. If you could see the scene as I do! Leah, you so utterly irate; Elhanan, you so contrite, and the . . . the culprit with her comical face." She laughed again, and both Leah and Elhanan joined her, delighted that Rachel felt well enough for such merriment.

With tension gone and the comedy of the situation enjoyed, the three of them began reasoned consideration of the matter. Rachel took the lead.

"While I appreciate your work on the fabric, Leah, I'm sure that through your marketplace contacts you can find another length of this weave, or even something better. Since the kid has been so thorough in her . . . redesign of this piece, why not add it to her bedding scraps. Perhaps, woman-like, she yearns for colorful finery."

Elhanan was overwhelmed by his mother's graciousness. His feeling of guilt, however, only worsened. "I'm sorry, Mother, so sorry. I would not have . . . I didn't dream that . . ."

Smiling, Rachel held her arms out toward her son. "I know you regret it, Elhanan, and you would have prevented it if possible. The damage done is really only inconvenience. Now come sit here." She patted the space beside her on the little bench. Still holding the goat, Elhanan gratefully took the offered seat. Rachel placed an arm around him, pulling him close; with the other hand she stroked the goat's face. "I can understand your love for her, Elhanan. What a comical little face she has! Her trust in you is obvious as well. I do think it wise, however, to plan safeguards

against future adventures. Otherwise, your pet may end in Leah's stew pot!" Again her laughter filled the garden.

"She would make poor stew, Mistress," Leah offered. "But perhaps a very small waterskin." It was evident that good humor had replaced the old servant woman's anger.

"Growth and healing naturally make your goat want ever-wider ranging. So I suggest that from now on you tie her close to her bed space before you leave for school each morning.

"Of course, Mother. I'll ask Tobias for a tether."

"Now, before I return to my room, it seems to me there is one more thing we should do."

Leah quickly moved forward to offer assistance. "And what is that, Mistress?"

"I believe it's time this creature be given a name. Merely calling her *goat* or *the goat* or *the kid* does little to identify her as a member of the family."

Leah spoke up quickly, her voice rueful yet edged with laughter. "It seems to me that *Tsar* would best fit the creature."

"Tsar? Why that, Leah?" Rachel asked, puzzled.

"Our schoolboy Elhanan here will recognize it as the old Hebrew word for *trouble*."

Due to the fuss created by the goat only moments before, Elhanan couldn't take offense. Instead, he realized how appropriate the name would be.

"Tsar it is! But, Mother, I'll work to guard against her *demonstrating* that definition from now on!"

Elhanan continued to sit quietly and hold his pet after Rachel and Leah had reentered the house. When the goat's head, with its yellow eyes, lifted to stare up into his face, the boy spoke. "Please, little one, won't you try to behave?" Then Elhanan placed Tsar in her bed—to which Leah had added the bright, tattered cloth—and pushed the unit tightly into place against the wall.

Joseph received the tale of the goat's afternoon escapade quite calmly as he and Elhanan sat together at their evening meal. Rachel evidently had forestalled the impatience or anger he might otherwise have shown. But, too, Elhanan sensed that his father's mind was focused elsewhere. That feeling was confirmed as man and boy later watched the day's end together in the garden.

"What relief to come back here to the peace of home and garden, Elhanan. The troubles outside these walls are growing every day. In the Council we spent hours today discussing the rising tide of thievery suffered by our people. Robbers are plaguing Jerusalem both in daylight and dark."

"Why the sudden increase, Father?"

"According to reports, there's an elite band of robbers newly formed. Their boldness and organization indicate a canny leader. Most troublesome, though, is that the robbers come from among our own people."

"Perhaps I can help—learn some details about the band, Father. Those in the streets seem to know things first."

"That's true. Any bit of information could prove to be a help. I'll be grateful for anything you can discover."

The following day, after school and stable work, Elhanan broached the subject of the robberies to Amplias.

"I've heard whispering of robbers." As he spoke, Amplias' fingers were counting his day's earnings. Pleased with the collection of coins, he dropped them into the leather pouch at his waist. "It's said that this band operates with special craftiness and cruelty."

"Whatever you can tell me may help all of the City by helping the Council, Amplias."

Amplias nodded. "In helping you I help myself as well. You Jews provide my living; so if robbers empty your pockets, the less I'll be able to do so!" Amplias grinned broadly as he spoke.

Elhanan chuckled. "We'd rather lose to your begging hands than to their robbing ones!"

Growing serious, Amplias said, "Word on the street is that the thieves feel safe plundering their own people rather than taking chances against the Romans."

"That's a choice cannily made," Elhanan murmured.

Amplias continued, "A name has also become connected to the group, though no family can be traced from it."

"And that name is?" prompted Elhanan.

"Barabbas."

"Barabbas." Elhanan repeated the name softly.

"It's said he has begun proclaiming his name to victims, saying he means to make the name famous."

"Wonderful ambition that!" Elhanan said sarcastically.

"But your people can thwart his plans when they learn his true identity, eh?"

Elhanan frowned, staring down the little street with unseeing eyes. "They'll surely try, Amplias. But . . . well . . . I'll pass along your information, and I thank you." With a determined effort Elhanan dragged his thoughts away from matters of thievery. "Now I must go. The shadows grow long, telling me that my own shadow must quickly fall across our courtyard entrance. Until tomorrow then." And with that, Elhanan briskly set out for home.

Once again, he had to face Maachah's blocking of his way. Somehow, though, his mental image of a hulking, faceless Barabbas harrying the City made the bully's challenge less fearsome. Elhanan halted, looking at his tormentor with a newly intense focus. The bigger boy sensed something amiss in his victim. He shifted his feet, assuming an even more threatening stance. "So now, Elhaynan, what is this stare supposed to mean? Your silly eyes are taking on the look of that miserable goat."

Elhanan interrupted. "I've just noticed something, Maachah."

The bully's face twisted in an ugly sneer. "Oh, have you now? And what might that be, my *little*, *scrawny* Elhaynan?"

"This spot where you confront me. It's carefully chosen, isn't it, Maachah? I thought it was the narrow passage that made you prefer it, in order to block my way. But today I see a greater reason. This is *around the corner* from your own house, eh, Maachah?"

Maachah's expression clouded. He thrust his jaw forward. "So what of that, Mouse?"

"In this spot, no one at your house can hear either how the mouse squeaks or how the rat screams."

A red flush rose in Maachah's face. He took a quick step toward Elhanan. "Rat! Why, you—"

"Maachah?" The call rang clear in the street; the bully froze. "Maachah, where are you?" The voice sounded louder. Then a short, stocky figure turned the corner. Maachah whirled, the abrupt change in body and attitude obvious. "Yes, Mama? Here I am."

Maachah's mother advanced on her son. She drew close, looking up into the boy's blushing face with a frown on her own. "I can see that you're here. But the question is why? You have duties in the house right now, don't you? You led me to believe that you were busy about those duties, yet now I find you here in the street. This is happening far too often of late, Maachah. This and other things that highly displease me. We are reaching a point at which your father must be informed." As she spoke, the little woman turned away and started back around the corner, displeasure evident in every line of her body. With a final, fierce glare in Elhanan's direction, Maachah followed her. The last thing the smaller boy heard as the duo disappeared around the corner was Maachah's whine, "But Mama . . ."

Elhanan's thoughts had returned to the robbery situation by the time he reached his own gate. He was so absorbed that he almost walked full force into Leah's broad back. He recoiled, and in the figure before him he saw for the second time in a span of moments great displeasure evident in a woman's bearing. Leah had not seen Elhanan; she was focused upon something in the garden. Elhanan slumped in disappointment as he heard her shout, "Faster, Tobias! Can't you catch that miserable creature? Let me stop guarding this gate . . . and come drive her out the gate and out of our lives!"

"Aunt Leah?" Elhanan spoke timidly.

"Ah, so here you are at last! A bit late for the excitement, I must say. Come in now and see your animal's latest means of amusement!"

Although the servant's angry threats made Elhanan's heart heavy with dread and worry, when he squeezed past Leah and caught sight of Tsar, he almost burst into hysterical laughter. For there, halfway up the steep face of the garden's rock formation, stood the little goat. Her head was cocked in curiosity as she watched Tobias's frantic attempts to lure or capture her. Actually, however, only one yellow eye observed the servant. The goat's left eye was covered by a small, broken pot with its rim hooked over her right horn nub. So capped, the kid looked for all the world like the mindless, crazily hatted fellow Elhanan occasionally met in the City streets. Generations of schoolboys had tormented the fellow by knocking off his multiple hats with tossed pebbles. Then they would flee in giggling terror as their victim roared after them and angrily retrieved his hats.

But this was no time to indulge his amusement over the likeness. "I'll get her, Leah," Elhanan assured the red-faced servant.

"Get her you should! She ought to be got into a bigger pot than that fine one she's ruined! Stew! It's only stew that creature is fit for!"

Elhanan dashed toward the rocks. Slipping out of his sandals, he passed Tobias and easily scaled the stone face, hands and feet finding familiar spots to aid his climb. Tsar stood on a tiny, high ledge, watching the boy's approach. She shook her head in an attempt to dislodge the pot; it clunked emptily against her skull but did not loosen. Although Elhanan quickly came within reach of the goat, getting the creature in hand and making the return trip down the rock face demanded coaxing, effort, and skill. At last, however, boy and goat reached level ground where Tobias was trying to calm his fuming wife. Leah's grumblings were only slightly lessened when Tobias and Elhanan had pried the pot off Tsar's head and found its broken piece inside.

"See, Leah, there's little harm done. Tobias can make it good as new. The pot just went on an unexpected journey, you might say," Elhanan tried to placate Leah.

"I might say, indeed! Unexpected journey, unexpected *everything*. That's what this . . . this creature has brought to our household! Chores get interrupted, order and quiet are destroyed—"

"And you therefore gain both exercise and excitement unknown here before Tsar's coming, isn't that so, Leah?" Rachel's soft voice interjected. All eyes turned to where she had appeared unexpectedly in the doorway.

"Mistress! I'm so sorry. But this creature . . ."

"I know, Leah, I know. It's evident that Tsar is again challenging your patience."

"Challenging! She threatens to destroy not only patience but sanity!" Leah's voice shook with frustration.

"Come, Leah. Help me to the garden seat if you will. Joseph is due home soon. I'll wait for him here tonight."

With the now hatless Tsar still held firmly in his arms, Elhanan followed the two women to the stone bench. When Rachel was seated and the servants had disappeared into the house, he settled cross-legged on the ground at his mother's feet. Conscience drove him to speak.

"I'm truly sorry, Mother, that again we disturbed your rest."

Rachel touched Elhanan's bent head. "Rest itself grows wearying, my son. Even Leah's shrieks of dismay can be welcome change from too much inaction."

Elhanan leaned in grateful silence against his mother's legs. "It's easy to see that Tsar makes your heart restful, Son. That adds to the quiet and health of my own heart." Rachel's voice came gently through the gathering darkness.

"We hope to see your complete return to health soon, Mother."

Rachel patted her son's shoulder. "Our home is filled with yearning for my healing, Elhanan. That cheers me, of course, since it speaks of love. Yet . . . the intensity of that yearning also weighs heavily upon me."

"But Mother," Elhanan protested, "we only want you to be well! Do you mean we shouldn't care?"

"No, no of course not. But perhaps it might be better for all of you—and for me—if my getting well were not so much . . . so great a *must*." Rachel's voice trailed off into silence.

Elhanan struggled to absorb his mother's words. He yearned to please her in every way possible, but he was baffled.

Rachel broke the moment with a short laugh. "But look at us, my son, moping here in the fading light when we should be happily anticipating your father's return. Let's not make him wish to flee again to the Council chambers!"

Elhanan looked up at his mother. She was haloed by the dying sunlight. Her features were indistinct, whether dimmed by the advancing darkness or because of the tears that rose to his eyes, he couldn't tell.

Chapter Six

When Joseph came home and saw Rachel waiting for him there in the garden rather than in the house, joy lit his face. Though Rachel ate little at their evening meal, she chatted brightly and was able to stay up for nearly an hour afterwards. Then Joseph and Leah took her to the bedroom.

Elhanan waited until after his mother retired to take Tsar from her bedding area so she could exercise. He enjoyed watching the little goat. Her antics clearly demonstrated her joy at being freed from her pen. At length Joseph came out of the house to join him.

"Your mother seemed improved this evening. How long had she been up before I came home?"

"We had been sitting here for some time, Father. She was pleased to be feeling better."

A great sigh came from Joseph. "Her sick bed is difficult for you and me, Elhanan, but it's much harder for your mother

herself. It's not in body only that she suffers. This wasting sickness also takes a great toll on her outward-reaching mind and her others-centered heart. Some women would relish retirement from activity and duty, but your mother hates it."

Elhanan nodded in agreement. He thought back sadly to the days when his mother had been constantly and happily busy, involved not only in caring for her own household but also in helping friends and acquaintances in needs of every kind.

"But we go over wearying ground by talking thus. In Jehovah's own good time surely the sickness will be past, and your mother will again be the moving hub around which our family wheel revolves."

Joseph's words and the intense emotion behind them reminded Elhanan of the earlier, puzzling discussion with his mother. He was greatly relieved, therefore, when his father changed the subject.

"Today's entire Council meeting was given over to speculation, conflicting reports, arguments, and suggestions about the plague of robberies."

"The streets echo with the same concerns."

"And you learned . . .?" Joseph prompted.

Elhanan was grateful he could relay Amplias' information to his father.

Furrows deepened between Joseph's brows as he listened. "How many men are thought to be involved?"

"Word is that the band is small."

Joseph nodded. "The fewer they are in number, the more easily they can move about the city, appearing and disappearing. There's less chance, too, of someone in the group making a careless slip which would betray them."

"But though the group is small, its leader seems unbelievably bold. Only yesterday it was said he'd begun boasting his identity in the very act of robbing! He calls himself Barabbas."

"Barabbas?" Joseph repeated. "An alias, surely?"

"It seems to be. No one has discovered any history or family connections."

"I'll pass all this along to the Council tomorrow. Perhaps as others bring in similar bits of information, we can construct a meaningful picture. But then, what to do with the picture? Even when and if he's identified, we're hampered both in protecting ourselves and in punishing the thieves because of our being under Roman rule. Clever fellow indeed, this Barabbas!"

Elhanan brightened with a thought. "But Father, since we Jews can't move against the thieves ourselves, why not set the Romans after them?"

Joseph shook his head. "To a certain extent, anything plaguing us *pleases* the Romans, Elhanan. The more we bleed, the weaker we are, and the less capable of challenging our captors."

"I think Captain Melzar is different. He doesn't seem to consider Jews to be soulless animals. Could I speak to him, Father?"

Joseph didn't reply at once. He gazed into the distance, his face thoughtful. When he spoke his words were measured and weighty. "Informing the captain of our troubles and asking for help would be a risky burden for your young shoulders. The captain might resent such a petition—even to the point of ending your employment."

Elhanan was jolted to silence. The very thought of forfeiting the horses' care stabbed him to the heart. But he knew such fear was selfish. His people's increased suffering because of the robbers demanded that he must think and act beyond his personal concerns.

"Ah, I see you leaped into your offer of help before you looked carefully to see where your leap might take you. You needn't risk your work for the captain, Son. You've already helped us by gathering information. I'll share it with the Council, and eventually our leaders will find a way to gain Roman help against this plague of robberies."

Elhanan drew a long breath, then he squared his shoulders. "But, Father, from everything you've told me before, official appeals almost always mean official rejection. But if I appeal to Captain Melzar on a personal level, it might win personal concern."

"What of the horses, Elhanan, should your Roman captain react harshly and deny you further access to his mounts?"

The boy's response came without hesitation. "Then, so be it. My loss can't be compared with what our people stand to suffer if the robberies continue and grow worse."

Joseph spoke through a constricted throat. "That's a manly choice, Elhanan." He smiled. "And now let's speak of more pleasant things. Tell me, first, how your lessons go at synagogue school." The two ended their time in the garden with a quiet discussion of an unusual interpretation of a Torah passage suggested that day by the rabbi.

Once in bed, however, Elhanan lay awake far into the night. In his mind the scene with his father alternated with varying imagined meetings with Captain Melzar. When at last he crossed the boundary between wakefulness and sleep, his bleak mental landscape still held sway. He moved heavily through dream encounters with Melzar shouting angrily at him . . . with Vicanor and Nicanor pelting him with stones . . . with his own tearful attempts to mount Lux or Flamma, only to fall as they reared and plunged away from him, their eyes wild.

Elhanan woke the next morning relieved to be free from his dreams, but weary in body from the night's poor sleep. Before leaving for his day at synagogue school and the stables, Elhanan took very special care to insure Tsar's daylong confinement. Glancing toward the house to be certain he was unobserved, he took the goat in his arms for a parting caress. "Please now, Tsar, behave yourself this day. Aunt Leah's patience has been stretched to the breaking point." He put his face close to the kid's head, smiling at the sensation of the soft-rough hair against his skin and the smell of milk on the baby animal's breath.

Synagogue school passed all too quickly for Elhanan's liking. For the first time since becoming Melzar's stableboy, he was reluctant to leave the classroom and head toward the Fortress Antonia. All the way through the bustling streets, he mentally rehearsed various ways to present the Barabbas problem to the Roman captain. One after another, he rejected each.

Once in the stable he worked quietly, glad that the twins chose not to make an appearance. He was far too distracted to deal with their high spirits. All was peaceful in the stable as he saddled the horses and on the exercise grounds as he put them through their routine. Even the stable courtyard afterwards was his alone as he watered the horses and led them back into their stalls. He was removing the saddle from Flamma, thinking that Melzar was, like his sons, otherwise occupied and kept from the stable, when he recognized his employer's tread on the stones of the corridor. His hands began to shake so badly that he had trouble putting the saddle on its wall peg. But the customary warmth of Melzar's voice calmed him.

"Ho there, Elhanan. I see you're finishing your day's work. I'm glad you didn't slip away before I came. I have your wages here."

"Thank you, sir. My weeks with the horses seem hardly to begin before they end."

"Wonderful! Ours is a happy arrangement indeed: you enjoy your work, and I appreciate your reliability and spirit." Melzar positioned himself so he could stroke both his horses. Their heads had appeared over the stall doors the moment their master spoke. "You, too, approve the care Elhanan gives, don't you, my friends? Your coats gleam, yet your muscles are firm and strong."

Elhanan was warmed by the praise. At the same time, dread coursed through him, dread of possibly losing his position if he made his intended appeal.

Giving Lux and Flamma each a final pat on the nose, the Roman moved slightly away from the stalls. Then he spoke again. "I've yet another task for you, if you'd favor my request."

"Sir?" Elhanan choked out the word, startled that Melzar was making a request before Elhanan could present his own.

"Tomorrow I'd like you to extend your usual time with us here. If your parents will allow it, I want you to visit our home."

Elhanan's amazement at the unexpected turn of events held him silent. Melzar continued, "Vicanor has injured his leg. Though the damage is minor, it demands careful tending lest it permanently affect his growing bones."

"I'm sorry to hear that, Captain. I wondered at the twins' absence."

Melzar chuckled. "I doubt the stable's quiet was entirely unpleasant. But to get on with my request, Vicanor has asked if you might come to the house. I've made it clear to him that such a visit depends entirely upon your parents' permission and your own wishes."

"I don't know what my father might decide, sir, but should he say yes, I'll be glad to come."

Melzar nodded, obviously pleased. "Then I'll ask tomorrow for your father's decision." With the matter so arranged, Melzar gave Elhanan his wages and left the stable yard. Elhanan's heart was far lighter as he completed his day's routine than when he had begun it. He had mixed feelings about the captain's request. He doubted his father would give him permission for the visit in a Roman home, yet somehow it seemed that Jehovah was presenting an opportunity that might make Captain Melzar more receptive to a plea for help against the band of robbers.

When he reentered Jerusalem's Jewish sector, he sensed that the ever-crowded streets were unusually alive. There was an indefinable spirit everywhere in the noisy, moving masses of people. He quickened his pace, eager to question Amplias. Reaching the spot his blind friend occupied, Elhanan plopped down beside him.

"I'm disappointed that you forego our game again today, Elhanan. Your approach demands no skillful listening at all."

"My own ears send me quickly to you, Amplias. Though I hear more chattering in the streets than usual and sense excitement, I don't know what gives rise to it all."

"Ah, good! How uninteresting it would be to learn so much each day without being able to pass the news along." Amplias' grin was bright in his dusky face.

Elhanan shook his head. "I wonder at your ability to gather so much information, since you hardly move from this spot at all."

"I don't need to move. The streets come to me. Those from every quarter pass my place here. And no matter how shameful or secret the topic, voices are never hushed near me, for people consider a beggar to be no more than a wall." Amplias chuckled knowingly. "What tales this wall could tell!"

"So, what can you tell me of today's hubbub, Amplias?"

"Ah, yes, that. It has to do with a man we've talked of earlier, a man said to be at once ordinary and yet not in the least ordinary."

Elhanan leaned forward to rest his chin in his hands, tantalized by Amplias' statement.

"Jesus is the name spoken, and Nazareth is said to be his native village."

"Ah—that name and village again," Elhanan said thoughtfully.

"Word persists—no, it grows—that this most ordinary man is doing most extraordinary things."

Elhanan sighed. "You know as well as I do, Amplias, that many claim supernatural powers. My father pointed one out to me recently—a strange-looking fellow, with wild eyes and tattered clothing. How he screeched and jumped about, waving his arms and babbling."

"But this Jesus is described as quiet," Amplias broke in, "wholly unexciting both in his appearance and manner. It's his performance that's otherwise."

"Yes?" Elhanan prompted.

"Well, he's teaching, as many others do, yet the report is that *everything* is unusual in the words of his lips and the works of his hands. People are exclaiming nearly as much over the man's compassion and wisdom as over his miracles." Amplias paused.

Elhanan held himself in check though he was impatient to hear more.

"This Nazarene goes about giving sight to the blind, hearing to the deaf, speech to the dumb, wholeness to cripples. Even, it's said, he looses those held captive by madness."

"But you know as well as I how reports can be exaggerated."

"Jesus' followers aren't marked by hysteria. There seems to be a quietness, a deep listening, in those who hear him teach. And as for the amazing works, people seem intent upon disbelieving—denying them. Some who have been healed are even hounded by those around them—mocked and challenged. But nothing can be disproved. Think of it! Nothing can be disproved. There seems to be no trickery involved."

"The Nazarene must simply be more clever than others who claim special powers."

Amplias sighed. "It must be so, yet who couldn't wish for someone who truly had the power to do such wonders."

Elhanan was stricken by the raw longing in Amplias' voice. And it kindled his imagination and gave him just the tiniest sensation of how desperately his blind friend must yearn toward a true miracle of healing. The totality of that longing was evident as Amplias' fingers went to the stone god at his throat and traced its shape with urgent fingers. Hating the reminder of the Roman boy's idolatry, yet held strongly in the grip of his imagined, desperate need, Elhanan came to a decision. "Why not put this fellow to the test?"

"You mean . . . you'd join those who throng him?"

"You and I together, Amplias."

Amplias was incredulous. "We?"

"How better to prove whether or not the Nazarene possesses special powers? Eyes blind from birth couldn't be tricked into seeing."

"And when nothing happens? When I return to my place of begging here on the street?"

"Then nothing has been lost, but we'll be able to contradict the Nazarene's claims and urge other seekers not to waste their time. Our test can serve the cause of many."

"When and how do you propose we do this?"

"We must find where he is. Can't you add that information to your store of knowledge, my friend?"

Amplias hesitated before answering. "General information comes easily, but particulars demand others' time and effort, which means payment. So we come to the end of your scheme before it even begins. School allowance and alms can't finance such a project. Let's forget the matter."

"The plan is sound and the motivation good, Amplias. The more I think about it, the more worthwhile it all seems. My father speaks often and sadly of my people's gullibility. Think how we could help to shield them against further trickery."

"And paying someone to trace the Nazarene's comings and goings? What of that, Elhanan? Will you join me here in begging so that we can double my earnings?"

"I needn't beg, Amplias. Nor do you need to increase your efforts. Hold out your hand." The blind boy did so, and Elhanan placed the small leather bag containing his wages in the open palm. A look of surprise crossed Amplias' face.

"The Roman captain is paying you well, Elhanan. But no. You've told me the reason you're caring for the horses. You mustn't spend your wage on anything but your mother's gift. I know how important that purchase is to you."

Elhanan shook his head. "Aye. But think, Amplias, if this Nazarene's power be true, and he gives you sight, there's promise of a gift for my mother far greater than beads of any color!"

"You mean *her* healing?" Amplias asked thoughtfully. "But if you pay to find the Nazarene, and we fail to reach him, or his powers prove empty, what then of your mother's gift of the necklace forfeited?"

Those thoughts and others raced through Elhanan's mind. He already faced possible loss of his employment by broaching the subject of Barabbas' gang to Melzar. With another delay in beginning payments, Laban might well take the beads from reserve. The man from Nazareth would likely prove powerless . . . and yet . . . and yet . . . Wasn't it worth all risks to pursue possible healing for his friend, and for his mother? "It's something I feel I have to do, Amplias. I—we—must try."

Amplias sighed. "Then it's agreed. I, too, risk a great deal, my friend."

Elhanan was drawn up short. "You? What do you risk, Amplias? Mine is the fee, mine the effort to take you to the man of Nazareth, mine the gift for my mother put in jeopardy."

"My risk is only one, yet it's great. The risk of a dream never known before. The dream of actually *seeing* that which I've only heard, or felt, or smelled! My going to the Nazarene and coming away still blind may to you seem no loss, Elhanan. But that's not the case. A dream undreamed brings neither pleasure nor pain, but a dream enjoyed only to be shattered by waking leaves the dreamer bereft."

Elhanan was glad that Amplias couldn't see his face. "Oh, Amplias. My mind went no further than my own personal concerns. I'm thoughtless—no, cruel—to ask that you give your eyes, as it were, to prove or disprove the Nazarene. Forgive me."

"There's nothing to forgive," Amplias assured him. "Each of us lives within the small world of self. In your lighted world you can't comprehend the dark any more than I'm able to imagine living in light. Let's agree simply that we're both risking something costly . . . and get on with the planning."

"I've spoken unwisely in this. The decision, the plan, is not mine to make. You and I must not think anything further until I ask my father. As a son, I'm under my father's authority; to act apart from his direction displeases Jehovah."

"Agreed. Had I a father, I'd gladly honor his leadership." As Amplias spoke those words, Elhanan again felt a pang of sympathy. The Roman boy was alone, isolated, in so many ways!

As he resumed his homeward trek, Elhanan's mind continued to be filled with thoughts of Amplias. How unlike he and the beggar were. And yet they had a connection with one another that surpassed what either experienced with those of his own kind.

He approached the spot where Laban the vendor customarily displayed his wares and was relieved to see it empty. Another explanation of deferred payment toward the blue beads would have been truly awful in his present state of mind. Likewise empty was the spot where Maachah habitually challenged him. As he passed it, Elhanan found himself engaged in unconscious prayer. "I thank and praise You, Jehovah, for so easing my path home today, knowing that at home there's to be challenge aplenty."

"Elhanan!" Startled to hear his name called, he turned, to see his father hurrying to catch up with him.

"Father. Am I late, or you early? I didn't think I'd spent so much time—"

"No, no. I'm returning early. Leah sent word that your mother was worse. I summoned the Greek physician whom Rachel favors. He's to meet me."

Cold clutched at Elhanan's heart. "But Mother seemed so much improved last night."

"She did indeed. Perhaps, feeling better, she was more active today than she should have been." They had entered the gate; the garden was quiet. Elhanan's eye fell upon Tsar. The little goat was standing, dejected, at the end of a thick tether. But Elhanan couldn't stop to respond to the appeal in the kid's eyes. His mind focused inside the house upon his mother.

The house, too, was quiet. Joseph and Elhanan paused just inside the door. Then, after bracing themselves, they moved together toward Rachel's bedroom. They found Tobias standing at the door of the room wringing his hands. Relief showed plainly in his face when he saw Joseph and Elhanan. "Aye, Master, how I've prayed that Jehovah would bring you home soon. The physician is here, but I know that Mistress Rachel longs for the two of you."

They entered Rachel's room. The boy's heart constricted as he saw his mother's motionless body making only a slight hump under the linen coverlet. But as the physician moved aside so Joseph and Elhanan could approach the bed, Rachel's eyes opened, and she smiled up into their faces.

"I'm sorry for the concern I've caused you. I begged Leah to wait, but she'd have none of it."

"And well that I wouldn't!" Leah moved forward out of the shadowed corner. "If you think Mistress Rachel looks poorly now, you should have seen her at midday. For too long I put off sending for you, Master Joseph!"

"Thank you, Leah. You did the right thing." Joseph looked down again at his wife. "Rachel, it's important to me to know at all times how it goes with you." He patted her shoulder gently, then spoke to Elhanan. "Son, stay here with your mother. I want a word with the physician." And motioning the Greek to follow, Joseph left the room.

Elhanan pulled a stool close beside his mother's bed. Rachel reached to take his hand. "I regret, Elhanan, this worry."

"Mother, don't tire yourself by talking. Father and I are here now. Just rest." In response, Rachel's eyes fluttered closed like a tired child's, and a gentle sigh came from her lips. As he sat holding his mother's hand, Elhanan yearned to hear what the physician was saying to Joseph. But the men were in the next room speaking in low tones. It was impossible to catch their words.

Later after Rachel had been settled for the night, father and son tried to eat the evening meal while Tobias and Leah hovered about them in gloomy, obvious concern.

Elhanan felt considerable relief from strain as he and Joseph went out into the garden. Though it was growing dark, he loosed

Tsar from her tether, and the little goat trotted merrily all over the garden, every move evidencing her delight in freedom.

After silently watching the goat's antics, Joseph spoke without turning toward Elhanan. "The physician's words are not encouraging."

Coldness again clutched Elhanan's midsection. "What . . . what does he say, Father?"

Joseph rose and walked jerkily back and forth as he replied, his broken movement echoing his broken thought expression. "He says—first of all—that Rachel's illness . . . her wasting . . . is a puzzlement to him. That . . . well, that of course means . . . he doesn't know what to do . . . what to tell us of her condition . . . its prospects."

"But, Father, he's a physician! How can he *not* know?"

Joseph drew a deep breath, then answered wearily. "I asked much the same thing. He said there are myriad human ills that lie beyond medical knowledge. When I prodded him with questions, he would only commit to his feeling that your mother is losing ground against this awful wasting thing that plagues her."

Both father and son fell silent, each wrestling with the physician's opinion and what it might mean.

At last Joseph roused himself. "But tell me, Elhanan, how was it today with the horses?"

"Fine, Father. In fact, Captain Melzar complimented my work, and he increased my pay!"

"That makes me proud. It's important that you work diligently. A sluggard is useless both to man and to Jehovah."

"But, Father, I had no chance to raise the question of the robber band. Instead, Captain Melzar made a request of *me*."

"That's an interesting turn of events! What did he ask of you?"

"One of his twins has hurt his leg, and, since the injury keeps him from the stables, the boy asks if I could visit him at home." Elhanan could read in his father's face both surprise and uncertainty. He waited, holding his breath, through the lengthy pause before Joseph spoke again.

"How long would this, or these, visits be, Son?"

"Not long. I'm to shorten my stable duties, so that my delay coming home would be slight."

"The captain mentioned those conditions himself?"

"Yes, Father. He also said that he'd understand if you choose not to let me go."

"Hmm. This Roman is surprising at every turn. I somehow trust his intention and his word. You may make the visits while the boy is confined. Who knows? Perhaps your going will even predispose the captain to our appeal."

"I thought of that even as he spoke, because the timing seemed so . . . so unusual. Now, Father, I have another request, but not from Captain Melzar."

"What!" There was good-humored mockery in Joseph's tone. "You take advantage of my agreeable mood, eh, Elhanan?"

Elhanan shook his head in denial. "No, but finding Mother's sickness worse today makes it impossible to delay my asking permission for this second . . . um . . . venture."

Joseph raised his eyebrows questioningly, but he said nothing.

"My friend from the streets tells me of the man called Jesus."

Joseph was quick in his response. "Ah yes, Jesus. The Council's discussion of him vies with concerns about the robberies."

"Well, according to Amplias—"

"Amplias? So your informative acquaintance has a Roman name."

Elhanan blushed. But a glance at his father's smiling face reassured him.

"Amplias is blind, a beggar, near my age. What he hears and tells me about this Jesus and his miraculous powers made me think of Mother's need to be healed."

"You'd have us take your mother to this Nazarene?" Astonishment was plain in Joseph's voice.

"No, no, Father. That is, not without being sure that he could help her. Amplias and I want to see the fellow ourselves—watch him, listen to him, and if what we see for ourselves makes clear that his power is real, we want to . . . to ask him to heal Amplias."

Joseph held Elhanan's gaze at length. Then he turned and moved slightly away. When he spoke, his words came with such quiet thoughtfulness that they could barely be heard. "Your street friend is blind, you say? Totally without sight?"

"Yes, Father. He was born blind."

"Then if Jesus were able to give him sight . . . there could be absolutely no question. His claims would have met the ultimate test."

"If the Nazarene proved genuine in his powers, then we could . . . we could arrange to take Mother to him."

Joseph's voice rasped with tightly held emotion. "A few days ago I would have thought your proposal ridiculous and refused it out of hand. But now . . ."

"But now?" Elhanan urged, his heart beating hard.

"But now, since talking with the physician, I feel ready to— I'm forced to reach toward anything hopeful." Joseph began pacing again, and Elhanan could see that his hands were balled into tight fists. "But how dare I put this huge task—this testing—into the hands of boys . . . of you and your friend."

Elhanan snatched at the thought just presented. "Boys are . . . we . . . are small, small enough to make our way through the crowds, small enough to get into places big people can't reach. And fast enough to get past bigger people who block one another's path."

A world of tension, of expectancy, and of doubt was in the long look that passed between father and son. Finally, opening and closing his hands to loosen their stiffness, Joseph slowly nodded his head. "Agreed. For the second time this evening, you petition successfully. And this for a much more important and demanding venture. You must promise, however, to wait until this Nazarene comes well into the City itself. I'll not have you chasing about the countryside in search of him."

"Yes, sir. I mean no, sir. I mean—"

"I understand what you mean, Elhanan. And I'll do what I can to help locate the fellow. Nicodemus tries to stay informed of Jesus' whereabouts, at least in the general sense." But Nicode— Uh, I believe it would be wiser to focus upon your goat right now than upon either Nicodemus or the Nazarene." Joseph pointed toward the garden's rock formation. Tsar was a quarter way up the stone face, and she was eyeing the expanse above her, obviously planning to climb higher.

"Tsar! No!" Elhanan shouted, and he bounded toward the climber. There followed a short pursuit that the kid seemed to consider a game. At last, however, Elhanan captured Tsar and carried her back toward Joseph.

"At least she didn't scale the rock *hatted* this time," Joseph laughed.

"No, and her audience is smaller. What blessing that Leah's not here to be reminded of her pot-become-goat-hat!"

"Tsar's taking to the heights shows us that she has had plenty of time to use all of the lower garden elevations. That in turn tells us it's time to sleep, Elhanan. We're both tired. And surely your pet has exhausted much of her energy too. Good night, my son. May Jehovah give you rest."

"Good night, Father. I'll be in as soon as I put Tsar to bed."

Joseph entered the house; Elhanan carried Tsar toward her bed. The kid lifted her head and nuzzled his neck, and he laughed at the familiar sensation. "Are you asking forgiveness for climbing the rocks, Tsar? Well, little one, I could wish for some of your climbing skill, for I'm about to scale some heights too—the stone-faced indifference of our Roman overlords. And beyond that lies a cliff of rumored miracles."

Tsar's response was a gentle, sleepy bleat. Elhanan gave her one final squeeze of affection, then put her to bed and made her housing secure for the night.

Chapter Seven

*T*he next day Elhanan hurried through his stable duties. Sensing his haste, both horses became nervous and obstinate—behavior unlike them to that point. It served as a learning experience for Elhanan. His contact with the horses here and with Tsar at home was teaching him of animals' perceptiveness and response to human beings. As he closed the stall door after finishing their grooming, Elhanan chuckled. "There. We're finished, but far more hastily than either you or I liked, eh? Forgive the rush, my friends, but—"

"But his employer makes the demand." Melzar's approach and completion of his thought so surprised Elhanan that he jumped. "Forgive me for startling you, Elhanan, but you were absorbed in conversation. No, don't look embarrassed."

Elhanan smiled ruefully. "I'm more and more in the habit of speaking to dumb beasts, Captain Melzar. Here with the horses and at home with my pet goat I seem to babble my thoughts and feelings."

Melzar nodded. "Animals make wonderful, attentive listeners, Elhanan, and they neither gossip nor argue. But now it's time to leave the horses and visit two small human beings who are impatient for your coming."

Since his own duties were completed for the day, Melzar himself took Elhanan from the Fortress Antonia a short distance into the Roman section of the City. The boy noticed immediately that the houses were not only larger here than in the Jewish sector but also much more ponderous in design. At length they entered a structure of great gray stones. Elhanan felt uncomfortable as he stepped through the doorway onto a smooth, polished marble floor. Two manservants appeared immediately, and under their quick and skillful hands Melzar changed from the familiar military leather and brass to soft, fine wool. Elhanan could not conceal his surprise at the transformation. Melzar laughed.

"So, Elhanan, did you think me always dressed in soldier garb? I treasure the moment each day when I can be rid of its weight and stiffness, believe me. But come, let me take you to see more of my nonmilitary life." He led the way through several rooms then paused in the doorway of a large atrium. "Meridia, Elhanan has been kind enough to come visit Vicanor." So saying, he moved aside, placed a hand on the boy's shoulder, and propelled him into the atrium.

Seated beside an elaborate fish pool was an auburn-haired woman. Near her, absorbed in various activities, were three girls. Elhanan guessed them to range in age from five to nine years, and he marveled at the girls' likeness to their mother.

"Welcome, Elhanan. We thank you for coming, don't we, girls?" In response, the three smaller auburn heads nodded, eyes wide as they examined the newcomer. "But we mustn't keep you from the purpose of your visit. Vicanor has been counting the minutes. Sabrina, show our visitor the way to the twins' room." The oldest daughter rose quickly and led Elhanan through several more rooms. Just as he was beginning to feel overwhelmed by the size of his employer's home, his guide stopped. Without a word she made it clear that he should enter the doorway she indicated. As he moved to do so, the little Roman girl turned and hurried back along the way they had come.

"Elhanan! You did come, you did!" Elhanan's feelings of awkwardness vanished as Nicanor dashed toward him, grabbed both hands, and dragged him toward where Vicanor lay on a low bedstead of gilded wood. As ever, the twins chattered incessantly, alternately finishing one another's sentences and asking questions. Somehow in the midst of it all Elhanan learned how Vicanor had injured his leg, how the Roman physician was treating it, and how soon the two expected to be back visiting the stable. It was an unstated assumption that Nicanor would not visit the stables again until his double could do so, as well.

Time with the Roman boys passed quickly. Elhanan was sitting on the floor beside the bed, helping Nicanor line up small carved wooden soldiers under Vicanor's direction, when the girl Sabrina appeared in the doorway.

"Boys, Father sends word that it's time for the visitor to go, lest he be late getting home." Elhanan rose quickly, bade the twins goodbye, and followed Sabrina back to the atrium. They found Melzar in laughing conversation with his wife and the two younger daughters.

"Ah, good. I see your visit left you unscathed. Yours is a hardy character indeed! Before you leave, Meridia has prepared a bit of refreshment for you." He held a small drinking bowl toward Elhanan. "Freshly squeezed grape juice should refresh you, both from your visit and for your journey home."

Elhanan drank quickly to quench a thirst he'd not been aware of having. The juice was sweet and cold. "Thank you, Captain," he said as he returned the empty cup.

"No, it's I who owe you thanks, or, I should say, we owe you thanks. I'm sure that Vicanor has enjoyed your visit. And bettered spirits eventually contribute to a bettered body, it seems to me."

"I hope so, Captain. I'm sorry to see Vicanor as he is, and I'm glad to do anything I can to help his recovery."

So began the altered schedule. As his visits to the Roman dwelling became routine, Elhanan found the people in the household to be much like those in his own. Their actions and tone of voice made it clear they were a considerate and affectionate family. Elhanan found himself thinking of them less as Romans and more as simply people. Too, he could not help being impressed by the captain's thoughtful, protective oversight of Elhanan's visits to the house. Although Melzar was seldom able to escort Elhanan from the Fortress stables to his house, he assigned one of his younger legionnaires to do so. Then, following the visit with the twins, an old household servant named Amiah accompanied Elhanan through the Roman sector, leaving him only after reaching that part of the City that was clearly Jewish.

Among the general population of Jerusalem there was so much of coming and going, so many Romans in the Jewish sector and Jews in the Roman, that Elhanan's trips between the two areas caused no curiosity. Elhanan was grateful that his activities went unnoticed. If his schoolmates learned of his unusual Roman connection, their coolness might become open hostility. An added benefit was that by returning home later each day, he also more often avoided Maachah's torments.

Several days after having begun the visits to Vicanor, Elhanan was hurrying toward home when he heard a familiar but unwelcome hailing.

"Ho, ho, ho there, Joseph's boy! Why do you hurry so, my young friend? Come, come, come. Come see again the pretties I keep for you."

Elhanan reluctantly complied, altering his course to stand before the old street vendor.

"Well, well, well. Why so unfriendly now, Joseph's boy? I do you great service to treat you with special favor in keeping certain blue beads for you, do I not?"

Elhanan nodded mute assent.

"So, so, so. Why then so hasty in your passing and so slow in your stopping?" The beady eyes squinted at Elhanan. "What, what, what? No tongue in your head either, Joseph's boy? Ha, with words or without, you tell me what you're about, my lad! Gone again, isn't it, the payment promised for the beads? Eh, eh?"

Again Elhanan nodded, his heart full of misery at the admission.

"And what did you spend your wages for this time, eh, Joseph's boy? Tell me, tell me now."

"It went . . . it's going . . ." Elhanan stammered.

"Yes, yes, yes? It went?"

"For my mother."

"You bought something else for her? Eh, eh? Some gift from someone else before the beads from faithful and patient old Laban?"

"No, no, Laban, not a gift. No purchase. But healing, hope for healing. That's why I've given the money."

"Healing!" Laban's exclamation was incredulous. "How, how, how?"

"There's a certain man from Nazareth. His name is Jesus."

"Yes, yes, yes. We've spoken of him before, but . . . Ah, you've paid this Jesus to heal your mother's illness?"

"No, I've not paid him, nor will I. But the tales of healing are so marvelous."

"Marvelous? Marvelous? Ridiculous, I'd say, not marvelous. Empty claims as have been made so many times before."

"Aye, Laban, such is my fear. And yet, if it were true, if this one did have the power to heal. Don't you see? The possibility for my mother."

"The possibility I see, Joseph's boy, that much I see. But still I don't see an explanation for the missing coins, *my* coins as promised payment. Right, right, right?"

"Yes, Laban. Promised, and I still promise to pay for the beads. But before beads, my mother needs healing." Elhanan's voice broke at the mention of his mother's desperate plight.

"Hrrumph!" was Laban's growled response. "So, so, so. As it's gone from my hand yet again, explain its going this time, if you will, boy."

"A test. It's gone for a testing. I have a friend, a blind friend who, like you, spends his days here in the streets. My wage will help us locate the Nazarene. And then we'll go to him, and my friend will ask to be healed."

"A waste, a total waste, most surely. The crowds around this imposter, if as large as they're said to be, will see to it that your friend's *body* is crushed along with his hope for healing. That's one reason I've not gone myself. Ah, ah, ah! I see! It would be a testing indeed. And of course you hope this Jesus fellow proves his miraculous power, so that your mother . . ."

"Yes! Oh, yes, Laban!"

The old head nodded gravely. "She worsens, then, I fear? That's why you choose to give your money for this test?"

"Aye, she worsens. And the physicians, even the Greek physician whose skill exceeds others', they say . . . he says . . ."

"So, so, so. But physicians can't know all, Joseph's boy, even those trained in Grecia. Don't lose heart." Laban flapped his hands at Elhanan. "Ah well, go, go, go on about your test. Laban the Foolish will keep the beads yet longer."

"Oh, Laban, I can't thank you enough!"

"True, true, true. You can't thank me enough, so thank me not at all. It's for her I do this—for your mother. The beads will even more delight a mother freed from her sickbed. So go on, Joseph's boy. Go on with your testing of this Jesus fellow. I, too, will be interested in what you learn."

Elhanan's relief was immense as he hurried away from the old vendor. He could not know that behind him Laban muttered, "Go, go, go, Joseph's boy. Poor, foolish Joseph's boy, spending money for nothing, while Laban's lovely beads could brighten an ailing mother's remaining days!"

That evening Nicodemus and Adina again came to visit. They entered by the garden gate rather than through the house, having heard of Rachel's worsening. After inquiring about her condition and offering encouraging words, Nicodemus sank onto the stone bench in obvious discouragement of his own. Joseph sat down beside his friend.

"What is it, Nicodemus, that troubles you? Our Council sessions have been so filled with business that you and I have not had opportunity to do more than greet one another in passing."

Nicodemus nodded glumly. "My current state of mind would make conversation less than enjoyable for you in any case, my friend."

"May I know your concern?"

"Mine is much like yours, Joseph, as both have to do with our wives."

"Has Pashura fallen ill? She seemed in the best of health the last time we were together."

Nicodemus heaved a great sigh. "Her health continues strong. It's her spirit that suffers. I would not have it so. Adina and I do all we can to please and cheer her, don't we, Daughter?"

"Father's forbearance grows daily, Uncle Joseph, yet Mother knows no pleasure or satisfaction in life," Adina responded.

Joseph spoke thoughtfully. "One of the great puzzles of mortal existence is the unseen part of these human selves. The spirit within each of us is both affected by and has influence upon things external. It seems to me that there are ills of spirit just as there are sicknesses of body."

"An interesting thought, Joseph. But how to medicate that which is within? Would there were a physician who could so minister. No price would be too great for his service and for his cure!"

"Don't you believe, Nicodemus, that all within us, however strong, painful, or confusing, is beyond our own reach in order that we might acknowledge our need for Jehovah? The words of the prophet Jeremiah have long impressed me, where he records Jehovah as saying, 'I the LORD search the heart, I try the reins . . .' How unlike our access to and knowledge of our inner selves! So then He Who searches and tests in perfect comprehension of His own creation must necessarily be the One Who can meet the inner need."

"Aye, your reasoning is sound. But when the inner need looms large within *another* person, what can a concerned outsider do to heal the malady?"

Elhanan's heartache for Nicodemus' evident frustration and weariness moved him to speak. "Can't that person petition Jehovah for healing an invisible sickness, just as we do for an illness of body, Uncle Nicodemus?"

Joseph nodded assent. "Whatever lies outside humanity's reach *must* be given over to Divine intervention."

Nicodemus was silent for a moment. Then he sighed and shook his head, his expression underlining his statement, "I regret, Joseph, that in my extremity of concern for Pashura's unhappiness and its effect upon our household, I neither fled to Jehovah in prayer myself nor encouraged Adina to do so. I'm a fine Councilor indeed! Busy about prescribing wise attitudes and actions for our people while missing the prescription for my own concerns."

Joseph smiled, nodding his head. "So do we all, Nicodemus, so do we all. In my personal Torah studies lately I've been impressed with Jehovah's oft-repeated injunction, 'Take heed to *thyself.*' It's not only easier to take heed to others' affairs; it's also much more comfortable, since the honest inward look always reveals our needs and failures."

When Nicodemus spoke again, his tone was firm. "Then, Adina, you and I will no longer regret your stepmother's problems and pity ourselves because of them; instead, we'll petition Jehovah in her behalf. My mind is much lightened. We owe you thanks for the insight we've found here tonight, Joseph."

Joseph shook his head. "My heart has pondered much since Rachel fell ill. If personal schooling can spill over and be helpful to you, it's simply of Jehovah's allowing and for His praise."

Nicodemus lifted his shoulders as if a weight had been removed from his mind and heart. He smiled toward Adina and Elhanan. "You young ones sit here far too long in the somberness of adult concerns. Hie you now; off with you to some younger and more enjoyable pursuits!"

Elhanan felt grateful for the release from tension, and he sensed a similar response in Adina. The two moved away from the grownups, drawn in silent unity toward Tsar's corner of the garden. The little goat greeted their approach with happy bleats.

"Tsar sounds like she's in a cave, Elhanan! What have you done with her?" Adina asked.

"She is in a cave, of sorts. Tobias has walled off her corner with two slabs of stone."

Adina laughed as they approached the strengthened pen. "A rich house indeed! How did she fall heir to a palace?"

"Quite by accident. Workers delivered several stone slabs here to the garden a fortnight ago. Tobias said that since they'd not been used otherwise to this point, he'd use them to build walls around Tsar."

"They enclose one rather unhappy resident, I'd say." Adina spoke as she looked down at Tsar.

Elhanan stepped up onto a small stone that held a greater one in place. Thus able to reach over the pen's side, he lifted Tsar out of the enclosure. The little goat's bleats changed immediately from plaintive complaint to contented greeting. "Better one unhappy resident alive in the corner here than either banished or boiled, as Leah threatens!" Carrying the goat, Elhanan led the way to a nearby bench.

Adina petted Tsar as the kid rested quietly in Elhanan's arms. "I could vow your goat smiles at you, Elhanan."

Elhanan laughed. "It does seem that her little face changes expression. But no doubt it's only our imagination. I like to make Leah fuss at me by claiming Tsar can think and feel."

"Do you really consider it so?"

"No, of course not. I know that Jehovah created man wholly apart from His animal creation. It's just that I . . . well, I . . ."

"You see in Tsar those things that help explain the special heart bond you've come to feel for her." Adina spoke quickly. "I don't think that's weak or foolish, Elhanan."

Elhanan, although grateful for Adina's understanding, could not speak his thanks. Instead, the two sat in friendly silence, both directing their attention to Tsar, who was beginning to wriggle in Elhanan's arms. All at once with a concerted effort, she twisted out of his grasp and leaped to the ground. Without a pause, she headed out into the open garden, her springing progress clearly signalling her delight to be free.

"Stay here, Adina. I'll catch her and come back." Elhanan ran after his pet. He was relieved that Tsar passed behind the bench where Joseph and Nicodemus sat, rather than in front, where she would have been disturbing them. He could tell by the men's lowered voices and physical tension that they were in a serious discussion. He quietly followed the little goat, missing in his first two attempts at capture as she took advantage of the garden's darkness. Finally, however, he snatched her up when she stopped to nibble flowers near the great stone wall that had been the scene of her earlier times of misbehavior. Then, with one hand firmly holding Tsar's mouth closed, he made another undetected passage behind the adults' bench.

Returning to where Adina waited, Elhanan told her about the test of Jesus he and Amplias were planning. Adina was wide-eyed as she listened. But before she could reply Joseph called to them.

"Elhanan . . . Adina . . . we'd like for you to come rejoin us."

"Coming, Father." He quickly returned Tsar to her enclosure. Joseph began speaking to Adina and Elhanan even before they were fully settled on the ground in front of the two men.

"Nicodemus and I have again been discussing the Nazarene, Jesus. Because you and I have already been considering his claims and thinking toward a confrontation, Elhanan, we thought it good you should hear." Joseph turned then to Nicodemus on the bench beside him. "You're a key player in this situation, my friend. Why don't you tell them?"

Elhanan could hardly believe what he heard as Nicodemus began to speak. "Joseph tells me of your plan to go with your street friend to Jesus with request for his healing, Elhanan. I recognize the challenges you face in doing so, and the uncertainties involved. But I would encourage you in your undertaking. In the months since I met with the Nazarene myself, I've thought of little else, and your father and I have repeatedly discussed the man's statements and his personage."

Elhanan nodded. "Father speaks, too, of your discussions. So then have you decided?"

"*Decided* is a word with too much finality in its meaning. Neither Joseph nor I have yet arrived at that point. But together and individually we are moving toward it. And I would have you know that our minds through searching the Torah and our hearts through engagement in prayer are drawn more and more toward the Nazarene rather than away from him."

As he took in Nicodemus' words Elhanan felt a shiver of excitement and wonder.

Adina responded to her father's statement, and the words she spoke could have been Elhanan's own. "Then there's reason more for hope than for doubt in Elhanan's seeking Jesus' healing of his friend?"

"Aye. That's the point these two older heads of ours have reached so far," Joseph said. One pair of younger eyes will see, and perhaps another pair of younger eyes will experience firsthand that which can further our discovery and decision."

The four of them fell silent for some time. At length, Nicodemus and Adina quietly took their leave; Joseph and Elhanan moved into the house and went to their separate rooms without further discussion. Elhanan felt full to bursting with the newness and uncertainties that had suddenly come into his existence. Somehow, the mysterious Nazarene stood more and more at the center of everything.

Chapter Eight

The following weeks became for Elhanan a blur of happenings. It was as if he were being swept along by some great, invisible force.

A brief three days after the nighttime discussion with Nicodemus and Adina, Elhanan had found an opportunity to speak to Melzar about the robberies that were plaguing the Jews. The Roman actually broached the subject himself. He had come to the stables to check with Elhanan about Lux's tender left hind foot.

"Hold his head steady there, Elhanan. Gentle though he is, prodded soreness could make Lux plunge or kick. That's right— talk to him, as well. Ahhh . . . whoa, whoa, boy. Here's the spot indeed. But I can see nothing. It must be a bruise." Melzar let the horse lower his hoof to the stable floor. "We did ride fast and hard last night, eh, fellow? I regret that you must pay with this hurt." Dusting his hands, the Roman moved with Elhanan out of the stable, and they began to make their way down the walkway together. "We had a wild, and a fruitless, ride last night, and the footing for the horses changed from moment to moment. It's a wonder all our mounts aren't lame today."

"Why did you have to ride so hard, Captain, if I may ask?" The moment the words were out of his mouth, Elhanan wished he hadn't spoken, fearing that his inquiry might be resented. But Melzar's quick reply put his worry to rest.

"We were called out three hours before dawn because of a disturbance in a section of the city occupied by your people." At sight of Elhanan's worried expression, Melzar hurried on. "There were hundreds gathered in the streets, but no rioting. It was more like a gigantic mourning. Our task was simply to disperse the crowd."

"But why did you have to intervene? We—my people—guard against doing anything that might bring reprisals," Elhanan protested.

"This was the first such occasion for several years. The former commander told me of one minor incident he and his troops had to handle, but he assured me that in general City life is orderly. That being the case, I made sure my men stayed calm throughout last night's exercise. After I dismounted and went among the people, urging them to speak, I was told that a robber band—made up not of our people, nor of foreigners, but rather of your own—is plundering Jewish neighborhoods."

Elhanan found it difficult to keep a quaver from his voice. His heart overflowed with gratitude that Jehovah had Himself brought the thievery to the Romans' attention. "Captain Melzar, my father says he has never seen our people more deeply hurt and angered than by this band of robbers."

Melzar nodded gravely. "I can imagine the frustration there must be, living in bondage to one's conquerors while being savaged by one's own kind!"

"My father speaks of these robbers as the ultimate traitors, exploiting our helplessness to prey on us. Should we band

together and try to capture the thieves, our purpose might be misunderstood."

"How long has this plunder been going on?"

Elhanan sighed. "I don't know exactly when the robberies began, but talk of them has been common in the streets for several months. At first the losses were minor. But the thieves have increased in daring. They not only seem to know when, where, and whom to strike, but they're also more and more vicious."

Melzar slowed his pace. "It seems to me that the Roman military should begin a search and ultimately mete out fitting punishment. Some say that whatever hurts your people helps us; but I think, instead, that what troubles your people ultimately troubles us."

Elhanan's heart lifted. "If you and your men could somehow rid us of this robber band, my people's gratitude would be great. Father says that the Council would spread news of your assistance throughout all Jewish sectors."

Melzar looked his surprise. "So your father has considered seeking Roman assistance? I was told before coming to Jerusalem that your people, though conquered, were so proud they would rather perish than establish any kind of accord with us."

Elhanan reddened, but he drew a long breath and weighed his words carefully as he spoke. "Many of our people are bitter, and some have formed vigilante groups. But Father believes that we ought to live in as great harmony as possible with you because Jehovah allows your authority over us. He urges that harmony in the Council."

"Your father is a man of wisdom. No wonder he's a member of your Council—the Sanhedrin it's called, isn't it? He's right. An uprising, even though it be directed toward the robbers, could create a downward spiral whose end none of us wants nor can even imagine. It seems that we who are peacemakers, howbeit from opposite sides of the situation, agree upon the needed solution. I find that interesting."

"Captain Melzar, some of us have been petitioning Jehovah for His direction and help. I believe He's giving it . . . through you."

Melzar's response was thoughtful. "If that be true, yours is a god quite unlike our war-loving deities. But whatever the case, you may tell your father that we'll begin a search for the thieves. Any details your people can contribute will be helpful."

"I can't thank—" Elhanan was cut short. They had arrived at the door of the Roman's house, and the doorway was filled with Melzar's daughters and Nicanor. They pounced on Elhanan and pulled him into the house for his accustomed visit.

On his way home at day's end, Elhanan learned from Amplias that word had come of Jesus' whereabouts. He was known to be in the City and had been most often seen in the poorer precincts and near the Temple. Suddenly the plan to challenge the Nazarene's power was no longer just an exciting thought of something future. The time was upon them, and Elhanan was shaken with uncertainty. But, pretending confidence, he parted from Amplias with "Tomorrow then, my friend. Tomorrow we'll go and discover the truth about this fellow!"

As Elhanan led Amplias through the bustling streets early the next morning, he thought back to the previous evening at home; although he and his father had, as was customary, taken their meal together, Elhanan remembered nothing of either conversation or food. The time he'd spent earlier with his mother had wrapped him in dismay. He replayed the scene in his mind.

He had gone to his mother's room as usual upon his arrival home. But rather than asking about his day at school and the stables, she immediately began talking about their garden.

"Elhanan, you've of course noticed the slabs of stone that have been in the garden for some time now."

"Yes, Mother. Tobias helped me use some of them to make Tsar's pen. The rest stay stacked where they were placed at first."

Rachel sighed. "While I'm glad your pet has a suitable house, I regret that the stones have *only* been used for that. Their original purpose was otherwise."

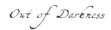

"You've never told me why they were brought in the first place, Mother. And I've failed to ask either you or Father. The slabs were so convenient for Tsar's pen that I never thought beyond that."

"I should have told you their purpose as soon as the stones were brought into the garden, but knowing how you . . . how we all feel about that special place, I didn't want to upset you."

"Upset me? I thought perhaps you wanted to have the slabs put around the fishpond, or—"

"No, they're not intended as paving stones. Or at least not primarily. They're to become . . . become part of other stone—our own stone."

"Our own?"

"The great rock face your little Tsar so loves to climb, Elhanan. For long years I've looked upon that escarpment as a marring of our garden—an unnecessary and unsightly part of a place otherwise lovely. But, of late, I've come to feel differently. And now I am thankful to Jehovah for the great outcropping. It provides a perfect place for an important and special addition to our garden."

Elhanan wondered at the halting way his mother was talking, and her pause at that point was long, prompting him to say, "A special addition?"

"Yes. I've asked your father if we can have workmen come and create a tomb."

"A tomb?" The words exploded from the boy's mouth.

Rachel reached out and gripped his hand hard. "Wait, Son. I know the word is hard, and the meaning behind it perhaps seems ugly. But I believe, instead, that Jehovah has provided us with unlooked-for opportunity. Few families are able to have the kind of arrangement for their family burial place our great garden stone affords."

"But Mother, I—"

"I know it's not just the thought of the stone itself that troubles you, but the sense of how the tomb might first be used—who may be the first to lie there."

All Elhanan could do was nod in numb, dumb acknowledgement.

His mother continued, "Few families have such a perfect natural setting in which to prepare for burying those they love. And, Son, hollowing the rock face will not mean its immediate use, or even the use of it soon. I've asked that the opening not be visible from the house, but placed toward the back of the escarpment. You know how I love our garden; I no more want it scarred or ugly or fearsome than you do. But in a way, adding the tomb to our land will put the seal of our permanence upon it. Although we've lived in Jerusalem for years, some still think of us as outsiders."

"I . . . I see. So it's not . . . it doesn't mean . . ."

"It means only what I've said. Can you bring yourself to accept the change? It means a great deal to me. In fact, I've been disappointed that the actual work of construction hasn't begun yet. Your father assures me he'll make contact again with the stone cutters."

Amplias' voice, and his hand tugging in restraint, brought Elhanan's mind from the remembered conversation with his mother to the present moment on Jerusalem's ever-busy streets.

"Elhanan, my friend, slow down, I pray you! You forget that you're dragging an eyeless wagon behind you! You may be making progress through the crowds unscathed; I, however, am jarring people on every side. If this goes on much longer, I'll raise such resentment in the streets that my hand will forever after remain empty of alms!"

"Forgive me, Amplias. My thoughts were still at home." Elhanan adjusted his gait accordingly, and he concentrated upon maneuvering Amplias more thoughtfully through the throngs.

"Ah, that's better, Elhanan, better. At the earlier pace I feared I might meet this Jesus person needing him to heal a battered body as well as unseeing eyes!"

"You make me ashamed in so many ways—especially your laughing response to difficulties."

Amplias shrugged. "Light is a better response to darkness than are clouds, it seems to me. And laughter is a thing of light, isn't it?"

Elhanan didn't reply, but he took a firmer grip on his friend's arm, and they moved along the streets toward the house where Jesus was said to be teaching. As they turned a corner, the suddenly swelling crowd made it clear that their information had been correct. It had not been easy for Elhanan to steer Amplias safely through the streets to this point, but now the task became almost impossible. The physical pressure of the tight-packed, jostling human mass was great, but the heart pressure was worse because of seeing those who made up the crowd. Amplias was only one of many blind; there were also numberless others who struggled forward in spite of obvious paralysis, injury, and illness. Some were alone, while others were attended by family members or servants. Then Elhanan was struck by something else—the silence of the crowd. Amplias spoke in a whisper beside him.

"Elhanan. The quietness! How can it be that I feel the crush of hundreds of people, yet I hear none of the noise that accompanies such a crowd?" Amplias' question underlined the wonder that had brought the pair to a standstill.

Elhanan responded in a whisper. "I don't know the why of it, Amplias. I only know it's so. It seems almost worshipful! But enough. We've not come here to think about the crowd, but rather to reach the one who draws them."

So the two boys began trying to advance through the throng. With determination and hard-held politeness, they inched forward. Their small size worked in their favor, allowing them to take advantage of openings in the shifting mass of humanity. As they inched forward they occasionally asked in a whisper exactly where Jesus was. The only information given was, "Ahead. In a house." Still, it seemed forever before they reached the house itself. Then, almost suddenly, they arrived at the front door. Elhanan's heart sank. People were not only pressed tightly against the outside wall, they were literally wedged into the doorway, as well. He gritted his teeth. He and Amplias had not wormed their way through the masses to this point just to stay outside.

Taking Amplias' hand, he began to inch sideways, his back flattened against the wall of the house. At length he felt the end of the house wall and the rough boards and iron hinges of a wooden gate. He drew Amplias closer. "We'll search out another entrance, my friend. Move quickly after me when I give the signal." Finishing his whispered instruction, Elhanan waited, watching the crowd to be sure that no one was interested in them. He reached behind him for the latch, and worked quietly with one hand to shift the iron bar from its stone slot. Then he tested the direction of the gate's swing by leaning his weight against the boards. He smiled to himself as he felt the gate move away from him without resistance.

"Aiyeeeee!" The wail sounded from far back in the crowd. The obvious pain it expressed caused everyone to turn toward the cry. It was the distraction Elhanan had been waiting for. "Now!" he hissed, and he rushed himself and Amplias through the gate, closing and latching it behind them in one smooth movement.

Amplias had fallen to his knees because of the sudden change from cobbled street to uneven ground. "I'm sorry, Amplias. I had to move fast to have us off the street and into the garden—into the *right* garden, I hope."

The blind boy was dusting himself off. "Don't apologize. We can just consider my sudden kneeling to be practice—"

"Practice? For what, my boy?" Both Elhanan and Amplias started. Though two pairs of eyes turned quickly toward the sound, of course only Elhanan could see that two men were there in the garden. One was seated on a shaded bench, the other standing beside it.

"Er, practice for kneeling in petition," Amplias responded hesitantly.

It was the man on his feet who spoke. His voice when it came again was tinged with amusement. "Is petition new to you?"

Amplias laughed shortly. "Hardly! Petition is a daily thing with me, sir; but I ordinarily sit while I beg."

Listening to the exchange, Elhanan's eyes were drawn to the second man. He sat unmoving, weariness evident in his posture. Yet he was intently focused on both Amplias and Elhanan.

"And why do you now need to kneel?"

"So that I seem authen—" Elhanan ended Amplias' words with a jab to the ribs.

"My friend only jests in speaking of practice. We're both weary from our efforts to get through the crush of people out there, and it makes him silly."

The speaker's eyes met those of his companion, and a nod of understanding passed between them. "The crush of people is wearying indeed. The garden is restful though."

"But we didn't come here to rest. We hope there's a way through the garden to the Nazarene who—" Amplias began.

"Oh, you seek Jesus?"

"Yes. Is it possible to reach him this way? The front of the house is hopelessly blocked, Elhanan says."

"It is possible to get *to* Jesus this way. What is it that you want *through* Jesus, should you reach him?"

Suddenly and strangely, Elhanan felt ashamed, deeply ashamed. He was not used to deceit. He had an immense urge to say to the strangers, "Exposure! We want to expose this Jesus fellow as a fraud by asking for Amplias' healing from blindness." But Amplias moved away from Elhanan's restraining hand. He took several steps toward the men.

"I want—I need—I want to plead with all my heart for healing from my blindness." Amplias' voice shook with such intense emotion that Elhanan's throat constricted, holding him silent.

"Your heart is in your words. I believe you would use eyesight faithfully and well."

"So, can you help me get to Jesus?" Amplias' voice was barely more than a whisper.

"Indeed. Come closer."

Amplias hesitated, then he slowly moved forward over the uneven ground. Elhanan made as if to help him, but the seated man motioned him back.

It was he who extended his hand toward the advancing blind boy. Amplias' hand made contact with the proffered one, and he moved a few steps more, then abruptly dropped to his knees. Elhanan gasped. From where he stood, he could see a portion of his friend's face lifted toward the man on the bench. Although he had spent long hours with Amplias, the blind boy's face had never before held the expression it did at that moment. Swirling emotions swept Elhanan: surprise, awe, love for his friend, and then anger. What did these fellows mean, detaining them here in the garden, keeping them from their intended purpose? How could they be so cruel as to have Amplias go through the motions that he must, surely, repeat when and if he finally reached Jesus?

"Amp—" he began. But again the seated stranger stopped him, this time simply with a look. Then the man's full attention was turned back to the blind boy kneeling before him. Reaching forward, he lightly touched Amplias' right eye, then his left. The Roman boy crumpled to the ground, great wracking sobs shaking his body. Elhanan rushed forward and knelt beside his friend. He looked up angrily into the face of the man on the garden bench. "What have you done? How can you . . ." There ended both Elhanan's protest and his conscious thinking. As his eyes met the eyes of the stranger, his heart was compressed as if by a giant hand. His breath rushed from him, and he was jolted backward. Through quivering lips he formed the question, "Who . . . who are you?"

The man rose from the bench, beckoned to his companion, and they began to move toward the house. But then the silent stranger paused. Looking piercingly at Elhanan, he said, "For judgment I am come into this world, that they who see not might see; and that they who see might be made blind."

It took a moment for Elhanan to collect himself enough to think again of Amplias. Seeing his friend still crumpled on the ground beside him, he reached out to touch his shoulder. There was no response. "Amplias, what's wrong? We must get up from here, get on with our search for the Nazarene fellow! This stranger has delayed us."

A muffled groan came from the huddle of rags that was his friend. Then Amplias slowly uncurled, wiping his face free of tears. "Search for the Nazarene? There's no further need to do that, Elhanan—for surely we found him."

"What are you saying? Did you strike your head as you fell?" Elhanan felt an awful coldness sweep over him. Surely Amplias had somehow injured himself. Or perhaps the trickster who'd held their attention the last few moments had cast some mesmerizing spell over the blind boy. Whatever the case, their day's adventure seemed suddenly to have ended. Without Amplias' clear thinking and artful imagination at work, they would not be able to carry through with their proposed confrontation. Elhanan sighed heavily. So much—so terribly much—had depended upon their plan! He shifted away from Amplias, resting his back disconsolately against the bench that had so recently held the destroyer of their plan. He must, of course, wait for Amplias to regain enough of his mental clarity to make their way back to their own part of the City. He certainly couldn't be left alone here. In his present state, he—

"Elhanan? My friend, you . . . you are . . . less than happy!"

Elhanan snorted with disgust. "Happy! Of course I'm less than happy. Our plan has come to nothing." He looked at Amplias and saw something indefinable in his bearing . . . the tilt of his head . . . the strange gleam in his eyes . . . a strange gleam . . . in . . . his . . . in his *eyes* . . . *his eyes*! The vacant expression—the fixed, unseeing focus—the milky opaqueness . . . they were gone! The eyes that looked back steadily into his were *seeing* eyes. Elhanan opened his mouth to speak, but he could only gape.

Amplias produced an indefinable noise, the sound coming from deep within him, as if from a well. The sound became a laugh as Elhanan continued to stare at him, dumbfounded. At last

Amplias' laughter pierced Elhanan's befuddlement, catching him up to echo the laughter. Soon the two boys were rocking with their merriment, slapping each other on the back, alternating between near-hysterical laughter and attempted recovery. Only when both finished gasping for breath and hugging themselves with the hurt of laughter-strained stomach muscles did they at last grow quiet.

Amplias, sitting on the ground, slowly lifted his head, his face turning higher and higher. "Aaaaahhh!" The long-drawn sound gave Elhanan a chill of excitement as he tried to imagine his friend's entrance into the world of sight. Hugging his knees to his chest, he watched those first moments of discovery. "So this is light! Not just warmth on my skin, but such brightness! And it's everywhere." Slowly his gaze moved around the garden. He reached out to feel the grass, gathered some in his hand and held the blades close, inspecting them. Then he scooped a bit of earth from the spot where he'd pulled the grass, sniffed it, and watched as he let it run through his fingers. Rising to his feet, he began a wondering inspection of the garden: the bench, shrubs, a tree, and flowers. He touched, smelled, patted, held his cheek against, or traced with his fingers those ordinary things that Elhanan had taken for granted until that moment.

Elhanan didn't speak until Amplias returned to where he sat. "I can't believe it! It—it's all so . . . What was he doing here in the garden? I thought him a seeker like us! Then when he called you to him and touched your eyes, I felt such anger!"

Amplias' reply was at first a whisper, as if the force needed to produce voice had failed him. "*You* cannot believe! The impossibility of it all is so enormous that I'll never—can never, so long as life may last—hope to believe . . . to understand . . . to begin to express the moments just past."

"I feel so . . . so *small* . . . so foolish to remember how we plotted . . . how we thought to snare and expose him as a fraud!"

Amplias nodded his agreement. "We were small. No. We *are* small. That's perhaps the clearest sensation I recall of my moments here with the Nazarene. As I knelt before him I felt that although my eyes couldn't see him, my heart was looking into the face of all that has been, or is, or ever will be."

Elhanan's throat tightened as Amplias spoke. His answer came in a hesitant rasp. "Perhaps you have done so, my friend. His claims are not only of power to heal, but from the first he has proclaimed himself to be our Messiah. If that be the case, he is assuredly all that you sensed, the one my people have longed for, the one sent of Jehovah."

From the moment he spoke those words, Elhanan felt as if he were suspended, somehow out of touch with his body and all that was around him. Yet, obviously, the two boys not only left the garden but also made their way through the streets toward home. Only as he reached to open the gate into their garden did Elhanan realize that he had brought Amplias with him. He stopped so abruptly that Amplias bumped into him.

His mother and father were sitting together on a bench, and Rachel was leaning much of her frail weight upon her husband. Yet her face held the joy that always came when she was able to visit her beloved garden. The two sat unspeaking, but somehow Elhanan hated the thought of disturbing their togetherness. Then Joseph caught sight of the two boys and beckoned them forward.

"Ho, here's our latecomer son, my dear. And not alone, I see."

The boys entered the garden and moved toward the adults. Amplias hung back, obviously not only reluctant to approach Elhanan's parents but also slowed by his fascinated examination of the trees, plants, and flowers. Elhanan felt his skin prickle as he realized the newness which must be assaulting his friend's eyes. There was almost an eeriness in trying to imagine what Amplias was experiencing in those moments.

"Father, Mother. This is my friend from— This is Amplias," Elhanan spoke as they halted before the bench.

Joseph responded "You're welcome here, Amplias."

"I'm honored to meet you, sir."

Rachel's head tilted questioningly at the intensity of Amplias' gaze, and Joseph suddenly stiffened. Elhanan knew his father had just remembered what the boys had planned, so he began his tale in a rush of words.

"Mother, Father. What I've just seen— What has just happened to Amplias is . . . was . . . We found . . . We came upon Jesus the Nazarene, but we didn't know. He called Amplias to him and bade me stay back. Yet I saw everything, all that happened when he—"

Amplias broke in. "My eyes! He touched my eyes!" Rachel frowned, not understanding. Aware as always of his mother's moods and responses, Elhanan again took up the tale.

"Jesus touched his eyes because Amplias was *blind*, Mother. In all his life he had never seen. He was born blind!"

"So you, and this, your Roman friend, carried out your intended testing, Elhanan!" Joseph said.

Rachel broke in, her voice faint and breathless. "And now you can *see*, Amplias? You truly see?"

"Indeed, impossible though it seems. All I had ever known was darkness. But at Jesus' touch suddenly there was light . . . and the world!" Again overwhelmed, Amplias' words choked off as tears coursed down his dark cheeks.

"You tell of wondrous things! Things to move the heart of any, as they do ours." Joseph tightened his arm around Rachel. "But I see that Tobias is coming, as do the evening shadows, to tell us it's time for us to eat."

Throughout the entire meal they continued to discuss Amplias' healing. Tobias and Leah, too, were caught up in the excited speculations about the Nazarene. Their serving of food slowed to a stop several times, but no one noticed, so intense was each person's interest in the subject of Jesus the Nazarene.

As supper ended, so did talk. It was as if each person had thrashed about through the sea of words, without ever reaching a shore of solid conclusion, but had chosen to rest on individual floating spars of thought. Then practical considerations came into focus. Family and servants alike were horrified at the thought of Amplias returning to the streets. A sleeping space was easily arranged for the Roman boy in Elhanan's room. The two young friends sat quietly together after Leah and Tobias had prepared the room. Elhanan felt overwhelmed in body as well as in mind by the day's experiences. Amplias gripped his arm. "Although we planned toward meeting the man of Nazareth, we didn't dream what the day would hold, did we, my friend?"

"It would be beyond anyone's imagining." Elhanan waited, sensing that Amplias wanted to say more.

"Through my years of blindness, the pictures I created in my mind were not only of the world according to my ears but also according to my heart's desire. Now, suddenly, after the touch of a hand upon my eyes, I still see two worlds . . ."

"Two worlds? How so?"

"The world as it is in the solid sense with all its newness, but also the world having to do with the heart. You, for instance, who have taken the time and made the effort to befriend me in spite of our unlikeness. And your parents who have . . ."

Embarrassed by Amplias' gratitude, Elhanan interrupted. "Enough of this, now! We're weary, and tiredness causes exaggeration. See how the dying candle's light creates shadows bigger than our real selves there on the wall. You have an entire city to see as yet, Amplias. Don't think me and my family to be overlarge; we're just the first people in your view.

"Very well, then. I'll stop trying to put my feelings into words." A quick grin lit Amplias' face. "In days past I could sense the direction of your thoughts simply by listening to your voice. Now there's the added dimension of seeing your face—which even in the candlelight shows that you're uneasy. So—good night. One thing, however, I will miss from our life before today . . ."

"Oh? And what's that?"

"Our game played so often on the street—with your ever-failing attempt to pass me!"

"Ha! Ever-failing!?" Elhanan punched Amplias in mock wrath. Both boys were laughing as they moved to their sleeping mats.

Despite his exhaustion, Elhanan couldn't sleep. Long after all the house had grown quiet, he rose, tiptoed past Amplias' sleeping form, and moved silently out of the house. Pale moonlight illuminated the garden. He crossed to Tsar's pen. As he peeped over the top, the little goat raised her head and bleated at him. "*Shhh . . .* Come, little one. I do apologize for missing our time together earlier this evening." He lifted Tsar over the barricade, moved to a bench, and sat with the kid cradled in his arms. "Hmm. It's evident you're not being mistreated, though I may sometimes miss caring for you, as I did tonight. In fact, you're obviously quite well fed!"

Tsar rubbed her head against Elhanan's chest. He responded by scratching behind her ears, and she leaned hard into his moving fingers. The boy lowered his head to utter the burden of his heart into the small, hairy ear. "What does it all mean, Tsar? Who is he, this Nazarene? Whatever it means, whoever he is, there is hope now—hope that my mother, like Amplias, can experience a miracle!

Chapter Nine

*A*mplias again tried to express his gratitude the following morning as he broke the night's fast with Elhanan's family. "I fear that my brain, and my heart, must surely burst in the wonder of all that has happened!"

Joseph nodded. "No doubt. We who are only onlookers stand in awe, unable to imagine what it means to you."

"The miracle of opened eyes will surely take a lifetime of adjustment. But there is a miracle of another sort which I find almost as overwhelming as the first." Amplias paused, twirling an empty grape stem.

"Another miracle? What did I miss, Amplias?"

"You missed nothing, Elhanan. In fact, you are yourself part of the second wonder. You, your parents—and, yes, your Uncle Tobias and Aunt Leah."

"What's this?" Upon hearing Amplias speak their names, Leah pulled her husband toward the four at the table, and they listened expectantly for Amplias to continue.

"Although Elhanan brought me here only last evening, a stranger to all but him, and a foreigner, you took me in!"

Joseph made a dismissive gesture. "There's nothing of miracle in that, Amplias. Jehovah instructs us to be hospitable."

"Yet to me it's beyond imagining, and I'll always be grateful for it."

Rachel reached across the table and put a hand on the Roman boy's arm. "We're happy to have you in our home, Amplias, and I trust you'll stay for however long we can be of help."

"I mustn't impose upon your generosity. My place is not here."

"But Amplias, you can't go back to begging," Elhanan protested.

"I'll not return to the streets as I left them. But I must go back to my own world. Staying here, I would remain a beggar, though of a different kind. This gift of sight imposes responsibility upon me."

"Your decision and its motivation speaks well of you, Amplias." Joseph nodded and smiled.

"But what will you do on the streets now?" Elhanan could not picture the Roman boy's future.

Amplias' infectious grin lit his face. "What will I do? A happy question! I can now choose. Choose from any number of possibilities, rather than be limited to begging!"

"How may I know where to find you?" Elhanan's voice held a plaintive note.

"That, of course, I can't answer, since I don't know where I may find myself." Amplias laughed, clapping his friend on the back. "But, could you avoid me in our game when I sat unseeing there in my place? No! And you'll no more be able to do so now!"

Elhanan and Amplias continued in the bantering tone the Roman boy had set, and the adults smiled at their playful exchange as they finished their meal.

Later the two boys left the house together, but their playfulness had ended. They moved side by side through the streets unspeaking. Their silence reflected the changes already experienced and the vast unknown that lay ahead.

As Elhanan went on to synagogue school after parting from Amplias at his old corner, he tried to sort through his tumbling thoughts. There were so many things and people to consider: Tsar and her constant threat to the garden; the old street vendor and the beautiful beads; Rachel's uncertain health; Amplias' miracle of sight; Nicodemus and Joseph's continuing contemplations. And over or behind everything there loomed a towering figure—Jesus, the man of Nazareth. It seemed he was coming closer . . . advancing somehow, toward all of them. People hurrying past muttered at having to avoid the suddenly stationary schoolboy.

Elhanan missed his daily game on the street with Amplias, but whenever they managed to meet, he enjoyed hearing his friend's tales of the street life he had formerly only sensed. Amplias had found employment running errands in both the Jewish and Roman sectors. As he told of his experiences, it was clear that while his feet and hands accomplished assigned tasks, his lips were employed to tell of Jesus' healing power.

Meanwhile, Elhanan's own employment had taken on a somewhat different character. Each time he reported for work he found Melzar's horses showing evidence of hard riding. The centurion did not explain; he simply said that both Flamma and Lux were getting sufficient exercise, so Elhanan's duties could be restricted to stable tasks. Since Vicanor's injury now allowed him to move about with splints on his leg, the twins again had become daily visitors. Though he missed riding, Elhanan was kept busy grooming, bathing, and feeding the horses, and the twins' chatter supplied amusement while he worked.

At home, too, there was change. Joseph and Nicodemus now met most evenings in the garden. Rachel stayed with them and took part in their discussions until she tired. Elhanan and Adina, though necessarily overseeing Tsar's exercising, also were drawn irresistibly to the adults' conversations. In many ways Elhanan felt that synagogue school had been extended into the garden, for the focus of the men's talk was the Torah. Specifically, they examined prophecies of the Messiah. Unlike lessons droned out in school, however, Elhanan found the men's talk as alive as the flowers and shrubs of the garden. One evening in particular would remain long in his memory.

"A king. He is to be a king, Joseph! Jeremiah stated it very plainly: 'Behold, the days come, saith the Lord, that I will raise unto David a righteous Branch, and a King shall reign and prosper, and shall execute judgment and justice in the earth.' Though he surely has a unique presence about him, Jesus has nothing of a king's power or personality." Nicodemus tapped the sheepskin scroll to emphasize his point.

"But is Messiah to be the kind of king you and I might expect? Jehovah intended Israel to be directly under his own leadership. He allowed them to have kings only because they begged to be ruled like other nations. Most of those rulers were far from admirable. They failed personally and led our people into sin. Then, too . . ." Joseph paused as he searched his own parchment. "Ah, here. In the Fifth Book of Moses. 'The Lord thy God will raise up unto thee a Prophet from among the midst of thee, of thy brethren, like unto me; unto him shall ye hearken.' Moses likens Messiah to himself. And Moses, being no king, must have been emphasizing the humanity of the Promised One."

Nicodemus shook his head. "But he is to reign. So he must be a king."

"Consider, though, how Jehovah Himself repeats the earlier description," Joseph pursued. "It comes very shortly after the passage I just read: 'I will raise them up a Prophet from among their brethren, like unto thee, and will put My words in his mouth; and he shall speak unto them all that I shall command him.' "

"Hmmm. You do have a point," Nicodemus conceded.

Rachel entered the discussion. "Leah and I have often discussed Jesus since he gave Amplias sight. People speak of Jesus as being from Nazareth, so Tobias and Leah are especially interested, since that's their home town as well. But a few days ago a visiting cousin told Tobias that the village of Nazareth, considering Jesus to be a trouble-maker and madman, is now publishing the fact that Jesus only spent his growing-up years there. He should rightly be called 'Jesus the Bethlehemite.' "

"Bethlehem! Are you sure Tobias said Bethlehem?" Nicodemus spoke eagerly.

Rachel nodded. "According to Tobias' cousin, the village leaders in Nazareth have uncovered irrefutable evidence—past census records. They're so intent upon disowning Jesus that they even employed scribes to copy the entire sheet of parchment which records the birth as being in Bethlehem."

"Ah! There, Joseph, that may be our best indicator yet!" Nicodemus' voice was charged with excitement.

"How so?"

"The prophecy of . . . hmmm . . . of Micah. Have you that parchment?" Nicodemus' agitation made him rise from his bench.

"Yes. It's in the house. Will you fetch it, Elhanan?" Joseph asked. Elhanan responded quickly, eager to learn what the writing might contain. Locating the prophecy of Micah among the numerous ones his father treasured, he hurried back to the garden and handed the parchment to Joseph.

"Thank you." Joseph spoke automatically, his attention clearly upon the parchment itself. "What prophecy do you seek herein, Nicodemus?"

"I know it by sight, but can't remember," Nicodemus answered.

"Here, then, my friend." And Joseph passed the parchment to Nicodemus.

There was silence while Nicodemus made his search, then he said, "Yes. It was a bit farther along in the manuscript than I remembered. Listen now. 'But thou, Bethlehem Ephrata, though thou be little among the thousands of Judah, yet out of thee shall he come forth unto me that is to be ruler in Israel: whose goings forth have been from of old, from everlasting.'"

"Bethlehem! Born in Bethlehem. So many things about Jesus echo the prophecies concerning Messiah." Joseph spoke softly into the gathering dark.

"Moreover," replied Nicodemus as he handed the parchment back to its owner, "it seems to me that the prophet Micah's declaration may hold the key to our earlier ponderings."

"How is that?" Joseph queried.

"I mean the Messiah's kingship. Bethlehem is not a kingly place. Therefore, and as you pointed out, his royalty may be a different sort from what we would expect. Somehow, my mind goes to the brass serpent in the wilderness. Whoever would have thought that Jehovah would use the form of a snake to cure snakebite! The form was of a common snake rather than something special—a serpent of brass saved the people from death by serpents' poison. So, the body created to house our eternally existent Messiah may be an ordinary human being born in a little place like Bethlehem!"

Joseph nodded, then he spoke slowly. "In form as a common man, that any and all of mankind might know him. And yet in truth the King of heaven."

Rachel turned to her husband, her eyes enormous in her pale countenance. "That is Jesus' very claim, isn't it, Joseph? You've told me of our leaders' mounting opposition against him, of charges that he blasphemes, because he says he is Jehovah come in the flesh!"

The evening's discussion ended abruptly at that point. Rachel, overwrought by the extended absence from her bed and the high level of excitement their talk had created, suddenly went limp. Joseph caught her before she could topple off the bench. There were hasty partings while Tobias and Leah took Rachel to her room.

Elhanan lay awake long after the house grew silent. Excited wondering about the Nazarene alternated with churning anxiety for his mother. Darkness was lifting from the eastern horizon before he slept.

Morning found Elhanan so tired that the day of synagogue school dragged. Even his chores with the horses failed to give him enjoyment. When he had finished his tasks in the stable, Vicanor and Nicanor proudly gave Elhanan the little salary pouch sent by their father. The weight of the coins, and the thought of their purpose, brought him the first real cheer of the day. Later, he brightened still more when he heard Amplias' voice. "Elhanan! Ho!"

He stopped, waiting for the Roman boy. Watching his approach, Elhanan felt surging joy for the miracle that had transformed his friend's life. As Amplias drew alongside, however, Elhanan was surprised to find him uncharacteristically gloomy. "What ails you, my friend?" he asked.

"Oh . . . nothing, really . . ."

"Amplias, you're not being truthful. I know you too well to be deceived."

Amplias shrugged. "My trouble is only . . . confusion, I suppose it would be called."

"Confusion about what?" Elhanan prodded. "Here, let's stop for a moment." The boys stepped off the cobbles and settled side by side on a broad stone step. "Now, as you in the past so often let me unburden my heart to you, I would do the same for you. It's the office of a friend."

Amplias did not reply at first. Chin in his hands, he sat watching the passersby. "Look at them, Elhanan. All those people, hurrying through Jerusalem's streets. Look at them!"

"Yes . . . I am looking at them, Amplias. But what of them? You've moved among them, seeing, for some days now. What is there today that you find unusual?"

"Not today. I mean, not just today. As I've told you, at first people gave mixed responses to my having sight; some rejoiced, some doubted, while others scorned. But the scorners have become fierce, accusing me and threatening those who believed. My newly opened eyes have shown me something very strange and . . . and painful."

Elhanan sensed that his friend needed quiet in which to order his thoughts. At last Amplias continued. "When I was blind, all those people belonged to me. Or I belonged to them. But no more. Now that I can see, they're making me— They treat me as an outcast."

"But why? How?"

"As to the why, I've come to think it must be fear. They fear before a miracle so evident, so provable, that their understanding balks facing the unknown. And as to the how, it's quite simple: they shun me. To them . . ." he waved an arm toward the thronging street, "to them I've become like a leper!"

"No, you must be misjudging."

Amplias raised a hand to halt Elhanan's blurted protest. "Misjudging!" He snorted the word. "This judge has been exceedingly patient, I can assure you. But the evidence—accumulated—has proven the case."

"Tell me, Amplias."

"Names—they call me names. *Liar. Thief. Deceiver.* They make charges. *You were never blind at all! You're a pretender— in league with the Nazarene. You're being paid to claim healing!* And they suspect me. *Are you a spy? What's your real identity? You say you're Roman. Why would you go to a Jew for healing?* On and on. No one wants me near, lest they somehow become contaminated."

"Oh, Amplias, I don't know what to say. It seems impossible that the opening of your eyes should close people's hearts. It's not fair!"

Amplias sighed and gave an exaggerated shrug. "We spoke together long ago of life's unfairness, didn't we? I should have kept my earlier, firm hold on reality. Instead, I expected . . . But expectations matter little in this world. Now I must decide what to do from this point."

"Come home with me, Amplias. You know that my father and mother welcomed you."

"You're kind, Elhanan, and your parents are wonderfully so. But it's your home, not mine. And, whether it be from pride or simply from habit, I must live independently, supported by my own efforts."

The two boys grew quiet, sunk in thought. Gradually, Elhanan realized that although Amplias' lips were silent, his stomach was not. It was producing a great many rumblings and gurglings. "Amplias, your stomach, I think, is trying to get your attention!"

"Oh. Well, yes, I . . ." Amplias spoke evasively and clasped his hands hard over his noisy mid-section, trying to quiet it.

"You're hungry! Only emptiness grumbles so. Didn't you break your night's fast? Have you eaten at all this day?"

"Er . . . no," Amplias rose quickly from the step and started to move away, but Elhanan caught his arm and forced him to sit again.

"I know you well, Amplias, and your stammering tongue and complaining stomach combine to tell of real hunger. It has been long since you ate, hasn't it?"

Amplias sighed, squirming under the pressure of Elhanan's insistent prodding. "It has been—a—some time."

Elhanan came to a quick decision. "Come," he said; and he pulled Amplias to his feet. "I'm hungry too, and the wait 'til time for the evening meal is long. On the next street we'll find a choice of foods." Amplias pulled back, but Elhanan was determined in his purpose. He realized in their brief physical tussle that his friend was actually weak from hunger. The knowledge made him both worried for Amplias and ashamed of his own inexperience with genuine hunger. Reaching the food sellers' stalls, Elhanan pulled Amplias into the first one and shoved him onto a bench at the back of the stall. Taking Melzar's purse of coins from his belt, he purchased a variety of foods. He set a heaping charger in front of the Roman boy, then sat down beside him. Amplias made short work of the food. Seeing it disappear so quickly made Elhanan's heart hurt for his friend's plight. When the last bite had been taken and the charger cleaned of every scrap, Amplias wiped his mouth on his sleeve and turned to Elhanan.

"Thank you. I owe you much for that meal, and the debt goes beyond money."

Elhanan shook his head. "You owe me nothing. I'm glad that I could purchase the food. Now, we must get back to our earlier discussion. If you'll not come home with me, what are you going to do to support yourself? What can you do?"

Amplias' restored grin came in answer to Elhanan's query. "These past minutes . . . while I consumed this feast," he pointed to the empty charger, "my mind was chewing on that question. And I've made a decision."

"Yes?"

"Since the people of Jerusalem won't accept the new Amplias, he'll go to the one who made him new. I'll go to Jesus and become his follower. There must be many practical things that need to be done in support of his teaching and healing—things that I can do, or help to do. Besides finding employment for my hands, there's also something I'm finding here." Amplias touched his chest. "I yearn to be with him, Elhanan. To learn more of him. It's as if . . . as if something important here inside depends upon him."

"But that means you'll go away from the City, Amplias!" Elhanan couldn't restrain the protest, though he felt ashamed of his selfishness.

"It's the only answer, Elhanan. There I can help . . . and be helped. Here, I'm helpless. And Jesus comes often to Jerusalem. You'll not be rid of me so easily, I assure you!" Amplias' voice held forced heartiness.

"Well, I . . . Oh well," Elhanan's concern turned from himself to focus on his friend. "You're not the fun you used to be, any-way, since our game in the streets has ended," Elhanan punched Amplias lightly.

The two boys parted in front of the food seller's stall. Neither could bring himself to pronounce words of farewell. Despite

Amplias' protests, Elhanan forced him to take the remaining coins of his hire. Then they walked in opposite directions down the street. Elhanan paused at the corner and turned to look back. But Amplias was gone. Resuming his way toward home, Elhanan kicked at rough places on the cobbles.

"Well, well, well. If it isn't Joseph's boy! Where is it you've been keeping yourself, eh? Poor old Laban, saving a certain pretty—" The vendor's voice startled Elhanan, and it made his heart sink, as well.

"Oh . . . good day to you, Laban, I . . ."

"Good day? Good day? Why such formality, Joseph's boy? Come here." Laban urged Elhanan toward him with voice and gesture, but Elhanan hung back, wishing intensely for some interruption or distraction. "Come, come, come. Now, up with your chin, and look me in the eye. Hmph. Miserable. That's how you look—miserable! Why, Joseph's boy?" The old man leaned across his display table, and the dark parchment of his face pushed close to Elhanan's. Then he cleared his throat. "Er . . . you . . . your mother. Is she . . .?"

"My mother?" Elhanan was startled by Laban's interpretation of his expression. "Oh, no, she has not—she continues ailing, and grows weaker, but . . ."

"Well then. What, what, what is the loss you mourn? For you do mourn, eh?"

In struggling to deny a sob's escape from his throat, Elhanan hiccoughed loudly. He clapped a hand over his mouth and held his breath, but the spasms continued.

The vendor suddenly howled in laughter. "Hee, hee, hee! Better than tears, now, aren't they, eh?"

"Yes (hic) . . . or no . . . I (hic) Ohhhh (hic)"

"Now then. What of the payment you've promised for your mother's beads, Joseph's boy? Hmmm?"

"I can't (hic) . . . It's gone. (hic) But I'll (hic) . . ."

"But, but, but! Old Laban grows weary of buts!"

"I couldn't help it! (hic) . . . Amplias was hungry (hic) . . . really hungry, because (hic) . . . he hasn't been able (hic) . . ."

"Amplias? Amplias? Who is this Amplias? And why should your money—no, why should *my* money—go to his feeding?"

"He is (hic) . . . he's my friend. He had nothing to eat (hic). And he's leaving (hic) . . . leaving the City (hic)."

"And leaving you, eh, Joseph's boy? And a friend must help a friend, eh? Nyaagh. Shoo, then. Shoo. Shoo. I'll not look for gold where there is none. No. Never mind. I can't translate hiccoughs. The beads will wait a while longer. No, shoo, I say!" And the old man flapped Elhanan away from his table.

As Elhanan moved on, his hiccoughs continued, and the tears he had restrained in front of Laban now fell to the dusty cobbles as he moved along the street. How his heart ached at the thought of losing Amplias. Everything had seemed so wonderful when the Nazarene took away his friend's blindness, yet now the healing had taken away his friend—his only friend.

When he reached home he found his mother confined to her bed due to her exertions the night before. Following a silent evening meal, he and Joseph retired to the garden. Tsar, though loosed from her corner, was less active than usual. She was content to stay close to Elhanan where he sat on the ground at his father's feet. But she persistently butted him on whatever part of his arms and legs she could reach.

"Even playfulness can cause hurt at times." As he spoke in response to Elhanan's obvious discomfort, Joseph tried unsuccessfully to turn the little goat's attention away from the boy and to himself, but Tsar would have none of it. "She's wholly your pet, my son, so both the pleasure and the pain attendant upon that fact are yours."

Elhanan winced yet again and shifted his position. "The thrustings with her head are more insistent each week. Surely her horns are set to break through the skin sometime soon." He rubbed his hand hard over the two hairy little lumps atop Tsar's head, and she pushed back blissfully against the pressure.

Joseph chuckled. "It will seem no time before your toy-like pet grows to be a fully-horned, heavy-bagged nanny. What will you do with her then, Elhanan?"

Elhanan made a face. "I don't like to think of her like that—all grown big and . . . and ugly."

"Oh, so your fondness for Tsar is colored by her attractiveness, eh? And your affection will wane as she loses her beauty?"

"No, I'll always love Tsar, but she'll be so different when full-grown!"

His father's voice lost its bantering note. "If what you feel for Tsar is genuine affection it will last, for you will care for what she *is* rather than for how she *looks*. That's a good lesson for a goat to teach a boy!"

It was not long before Joseph spoke of being weary from his long day in the Council room. He made as if to rise from the bench.

"Father, I . . . I wanted to ask you something."

Joseph settled himself again. "Of course. What is it, Son?"

"I wonder . . . I want . . . I'm afraid, Father, as I see Mother growing so weak. And now, each day when I come home from school I see, there"—he gestured toward the growing accumulation of stonecutters' tools—"the preparations for our family tomb."

Joseph nodded. "I know. Although I myself gave the order for the tomb to be dug, I try not to think about it. It would not be planned except for your mother's insistence. But even without the tomb, it would be impossible not to fear for her, Elhanan. We both, you and I, are able to see the worsening that Rachel tries to deny in word and action."

"So, why don't we . . . can't we, please . . . take her to Jesus?" Elhanan tried to keep an anxious quaking out of his voice.

"How I wish it could be that simple." Joseph turned away from Elhanan as he spoke.

"We know now that he can heal, Father. We've seen that proven. He opened Amplias' blind eyes! Many are going to him for healing of every sort."

"Many are going, indeed, Elhanan. Most of those going, however, nearly all are people who . . . They aren't . . ."

"Aren't what, Father?"

Joseph shifted uncomfortably on the bench. "The people who seek openly to the Nazarene are not . . . not the leaders of our people, but commoners. The ones who throng him are villagers, and merchants, and poor people. Those like us, like your Uncle Nicodemus and me . . ."

"Councilors?"

"Well, yes. Or others who have leadership. They . . . we . . . It's dangerous."

"How can it be dangerous, Father, to seek the Nazarene's help?"

"I assure you, Son, there's danger now even in speaking favorably of Jesus in high circles. The more the multitudes flock to the Nazarene, the angrier those in leadership become."

"But why? All of Jerusalem is excited about him . . . about his miracles."

"*Excited* is a word that can be used in different ways, Elhanan. It's true that all of Jerusalem, indeed all the country, is excited over the Nazarene. But in our circles the excitement is greatest in the negative sense."

"So something might happen to you if you took Mother to Jesus? Amplias tells me there are some rumblings against the Nazarene among people in the streets, but . . ."

"*Something* would happen indeed, and there's no way to tell what it might be! There is ever-greater suspicious watchfulness—and reprisals."

"But if he could really heal Mother . . ."

"I now believe that the *if* applies not to his power, but to his choosing. Nicodemus and I both believe that Jesus has the power of Jehovah to heal. In fact, we're coming more and more to believe that his power is not transferred, but is, rather, original."

Elhanan met his father's statement with a blank expression. Joseph bent toward his son before proceeding. "Only Jehovah Himself has original power, Elhanan."

"Jehovah Himself!" Elhanan blurted it with such sudden loudness that Tsar, dozing on his lap, jumped. "But that means . . . you think . . . you and Uncle Nicodemus believe . . ."

"We're increasingly of the belief that Jesus is indeed the Messiah—Jehovah come down to us as a man."

Elhanan had witnessed his father and uncle searching for confirmation of Jesus' authenticity. He'd heard them increasingly link the Nazarene's name with *Messiah*. But to think that the quiet man he'd met in the garden actually was Jehovah incarnate! The concept was too big, too powerful to take in. He would have to think, think deeply, and long. But for now, if it was true, and Jesus really did possess Jehovah's power, not just in part but in whole . . . "But then, Father, the Nazarene can most certainly heal Mother!"

His father held silent a moment. "As I said earlier, Elhanan, I believe that to be true. I have no question as to Jesus' power to heal her of her sickness. But there is yet a great chasm of uncertainty in his *choosing* to do so."

"I don't understand."

"Elhanan, the more I've grown to believe Jesus' authenticity, the more I've yearned for his healing touch upon your mother. But think with me a moment. Consider the day you took Amplias to Jesus. You found him not inside the house, where you thought he'd be, but rather in the garden behind the house, eh?"

Elhanan nodded, and he pictured that moment in his mind.

"Well then, think further. While Jesus spent those moments with you and Amplias, who was it that he did *not* heal? He cleanses and cures not throngs, but individuals. And just as surely as he reaches toward one, he must of necessity reach past or have his back to some other one. Do you see?"

Again Elhanan nodded, though more slowly this time.

"So, then, if we took Rachel to Jesus, publicly risking reputation and position, and Jesus healed her, I would gladly suffer whatever ostracism or reprimand might result. But if we took her so, and for whatever reason the Nazarene did not reach toward her, all would be lost. A man must count the cost of his actions, Elhanan. In this proposed action the cost is too high; the possible loss too great."

Elhanan could say nothing. He swallowed over a great lump in his throat.

Joseph reached out, took the boy's chin in his hand, and tilted his head so their eyes met. "All I can do, what I'm trying to do, is somehow take your mother to the Nazarene in other than a public way. Somehow, sometime—at night. Remember, Elhanan, Nicodemus already found Jesus in just such a secret manner once. We can also, I believe, do so again. But such an undertaking demands numberless details aligning perfectly. Pray. Pray diligently that I may be able to create such an alignment, Elhanan."

The following days flowed seamlessly one into another. Each evening Elhanan inquired of his father whether a time and means had been chosen for taking Rachel to Jesus. The answer was always negative. Joseph's voice had a weary finality as he spoke. Elhanan felt all of his internal self caught up in concern for his mother and rising frustration over the thwarted plan for her healing. He knew assuredly that his father loved Rachel deeply. How, then, could he accept such delay that might lead to her death?

Elhanan's inwardness was so intense that life's routine happenings were like waters swirling around a rock. They affected only the surface of his being, while all within remained untouched.

So it was that Maachah's snarled interruption to an afternoon's journey home caused Elhanan not the slightest jolt. The lack of response infuriated the bully. "Halt, Mouse! How dare you try to ignore me!" Maachah moved quickly, blocking Elhanan's way with his bulk.

"What do you want, Maachah?" Elhanan said it calmly, weariness of soul making his words a monotone.

"What do I want? I want nothing from *you*, miserable squealer!" Maachah glared, and his breath came heavily.

"Good. Then let me pass."

"Why, you scrawny—" He lunged at Elhanan, slamming into him with his full weight. Elhanan fell backwards, striking his head hard on the cobbles. Pain shot through his head, and darkness crowded at the edges of his sight. He could hear jumbled words, feel Maachah's pummeling fists on neck, chest, and arms. But he only sought to protect his face from the onslaught; he didn't fight back. It was as if the battering of his body merely echoed an assault that had already taken place inside him.

"Nyaaagh . . . get up and go home, Rodent," Maachah panted. "You're not even worth my blows. Next time try to work up a bit of muscle, won't you? Ha, ha, ha. A mouse rug. That's what you are. A limp mouse rug lying there. I should walk on you! But I won't. Not this time. Go home, Rodent!" Maachah moved away, running his hand through his hair to correct its disarray. With a final, scornful look back at his prone victim, he rounded the corner toward his own house.

Elhanan lay unmoving for a long moment. He hurt everywhere from Maachah's beating, but the pain in his head had decreased to a dull, throbbing ache. He slowly rose to his knees. And then the tears came, borne on great, shaking sobs. It was not hurt of body for which he cried, but hurt of heart. It was not Maachah's fists but life's cruel jabs he found agonizing—Amplias moving out of the City and his mother moving toward the garden tomb.

Chapter Ten

The following day, Elhanan's soreness from Maachah's battering affected his entire body. The pain of his heart continued as well. Synagogue school was miserable. Two instructors scolded him for inattention, and a group of classmates cornered him to mock his scratched, swollen face. Their jeers made Elhanan grateful that in the garden's darkness and the house's lamplight last evening he'd managed to hide the injuries from his family.

At last he was able to go to the Fortress Antonia, and he did so with great relief. He found Captain Melzar standing in the stable yard. Hearing Elhanan's sandals on the cobbles, the Roman turned quickly toward him.

"Ah, Elhanan—" he stopped short, staring at the boy's face. Elhanan made no move to hide the marks of Maachah's cruelty. He simply stood before Melzar, shoulders drooping. "I was about to say, Elhanan, that I've already had someone do your job today.

Oh, feel free to stay with the horses as long as you'd like, but this can be a pleasure visit for you. The pair of them worked especially hard last night, so they needed early attention. Now, before I go back to my ever-plaguing parchments, come sit with me here on the well curb."

Reluctantly, Elhanan followed Melzar, and the two seated themselves. "I see that all is not well with you, my young friend. May I help?"

Elhanan shook his head.

"Well, then, may I at least hear how it happened?" Melzar's tone was so kind that Elhanan told him the story of Maachah's latest attack. The Roman asked questions at several points until he had learned the entire story of the bully's behavior.

When Elhanan had finished, Melzar sat quietly for a moment. "Your— This Maachah fellow must be one of those who seem to over-populate the world, Elhanan. I meet many like him, in all walks of life. They thrive on cruelty and have twisted minds. Be that as it may, they need to be . . . discouraged . . . as early as possible. I think it's time this Maachah should receive a bit of practical schooling."

Elhanan slowly lifted his head as Captain Melzar spoke, feeling that there might be hope against Maachah's torments. Melzar continued, "Not long ago you did extra service for me. You paid regular visits to our home and encouraged Vicanor toward healing. Such kindness can't be repaid with money. So what I propose is this: there is a young recruit in my company with military skills that are out of the ordinary. I've seen them demonstrated. Although they're unusual, they're effective, especially when facing a larger opponent in hand-to-hand combat. Would you be interested in a brief training period under this fellow?"

"Oh, yes, sir!" Elhanan exclaimed.

Melzar smiled at the boy's eager response. "Good. I'll instruct the recruit to meet you tomorrow on the exercise grounds. While the horses don't need it due to our nightly enterprise, your training there can fit you for a different kind of enterprise, eh?"

After Melzar left the stables, Elhanan used his newly freed work time to oil and polish the leather harness pieces, all the while imagining what it might be like to face Maachah one day with the kind of skill that would undo his tormentor.

The next evening a young Roman soldier stood waiting on the exercise grounds when Elhanan arrived from synagogue school. The initial awkwardness of their meeting passed quickly. The instructor, whose name was Junius, was slender in build and genial in nature. From the first, it was evident that he enjoyed sharing his skill. Since Elhanan still showed the effects of Maachah's battering, Junius also showed grim determination to make his student successful.

Just as in learning to care for Melzar's horses, learning to protect himself physically was something entirely new. Elhanan had never known anyone among the Jews who thought in terms of combat, either personally or militarily. He was relieved that the training emphasis was not upon attack. Rather, the entire method consisted of quickness, agility, and strategic use of balance and counterbalance for self-protection.

Their first session was filled with Junius' verbal instruction. In the second he had Elhanan repeatedly copy body positions and moves while the teacher criticized. On the third evening Junius brought another young soldier with him. While the second soldier pretended to be an opponent, the instructor demonstrated how to counter different kinds of attack. Finally, on the fourth evening, Elhanan had to do battle with Junius. Each daily lesson thereafter was made up of seemingly endless repetitions, until all Elhanan's responses were quick and smooth. After several weeks of lessons, Junius and Elhanan laughed together when the teacher cried, "Course completed!"—because the Roman lay flat on the ground, successfully pinned down by his student.

"Thank you, Junius, for your patient teaching," Elhanan said as he extended his hand to help the trainer rise.

"I accept your thanks for the teaching, but not for patience, since none was needed. You've been an apt learner. I'll miss our sessions."

"So will I," Elhanan said.

Junius dusted himself off and made as if to leave. Then he paused, grinning. "I only wish I could be present to watch the next time your bully confronts you. Fare you well. Keep your defensive skills honed. You never know when or how much you may be called upon to use them . . . long after you've convinced your present enemy to retire from combat!" And then he was gone from the stable yard.

Elhanan eagerly hoped to meet Maachah between the Fortress Antonia and home. But the bully did not appear. Elhanan chuckled, realizing how disappointed he was, in contrast to the dread he'd always felt in the past. Looking back over the months, he knew that his efforts had all been for peace with Maachah. But the bigger boy would have none of it, so Elhanan now looked forward to confrontation.

As he entered the garden gate at home he halted, open-mouthed. A great change had taken place since morning. The rocky outcropping that had so delighted Tsar in her antics now bore a great scar across its face. Much of the jagged surface had been cut away and smoothed. In the center of the reworked area was a low doorway with hollow darkness beyond.

The tomb! It was the tomb—or its beginning—that Rachel so desired for their garden. A great, quivering coldness swept through Elhanan.

Tobias emerged from the house. Seeing the boy staring, unmoving, at the stonecutter's work, he moved quickly toward him. "We weren't told ahead of time when the work would be started, Elhanan, or we would have prepared you. The stonecutters appeared this morning shortly after you'd left for school."

Elhanan gulped. His voice squeaked unnaturally as he said, "It's so *big*, Uncle Tobias! It takes up so much of the rock. The garden! The garden seems so different with . . . this . . ." He gestured toward the tomb.

"It's to be bigger still, I fear. The stonecutter and his crew are to return. They say that to complete their work, they'll enlarge and smooth the inside, put in some marble slabs, then carve a sealing stone from that great hunk lying there. There's also to be a trough cut—a channel so the sealing stone can be moved."

"Awful. It's awful, isn't it, Uncle Tobias? How could my mother want to . . . to ruin the garden she so loves?"

"Her love for the garden is unchanged, Elhanan. She, somehow, considers this an enhancement."

The boy pulled away from the old servant and fled into the house. But once inside he realized there was no escape. Now he would have to face his mother. He looked in silent appeal to Aunt Leah, where she stood working at the table. Sighing, the big serving woman moved toward him. "Go to her, boy. Your mother this lifelong day has worried over your shock."

Elhanan could only respond by nodding numbly. He turned away from Leah, willing his feet to move toward his mother's bedroom. He halted in the doorway. "Mama, I . . ." Voice and words failed him.

Rachel extended her hand. "Elhanan. Son. You've seen . . . You saw . . . the garden. I . . . Come to me, Elhahan. Sit here as in other days."

Silence filled the room as the boy moved reluctantly to take his seat beside the bed. Rachel's thin hand closed tightly over his fisted one. "The stonecutters came all unannounced, Son. Had we known, we would have told you. Warned you."

As earlier with Leah, Elhanan could only nod. Although he ached at the pleading in his mother's eyes, he was helpless to form words to express the awfulness inside him.

"Now that it's here—done or nearly done, I know that the change—the presence of the tomb—must seem to you a terrible marring. I regret that, my son. Regret it greatly. I don't ask for your heart to change, except enough to honor my heart's yearning."

"But, Mama. A tomb! A tomb in our beautiful garden!"

"A tomb, it's true, can never be beautiful. Death stands throughout time as a tribute to Satan's enmity. And yet, there is this, Elhanan: death began in a garden, did it not?"

Again Elhanan nodded, knowing well the story of Eden's sin-shattered glories.

"Death is, then, a part of all that's otherwise beautiful in life. It cannot be avoided or denied. Isn't it better and wiser, therefore, to accept the reality and at least beautify its *setting*?"

"But, Mama, with you ill, the tomb . . . it frightens me."

"That very fear is one reason I asked that the sepulcher become a part of the garden, Son. You're shocked by its sudden appearance. The shock of my . . . leaving you . . . without a time of preparation, would be far worse."

"Your leaving may not . . . Father and I are trying . . ."

Rachel sighed. "I know that you're thinking now of resorting to the Nazarene for my healing. But as your father has explained, there are many obstacles, Elhanan."

"No more than there were for Amplias, Mother!"

Rachel shook her head. "When you and Amplias sought the Nazarene, you could make a bold, direct, daylight approach. In my case, there is much to hinder. I could neither walk the distance, nor well endure the jostling of a conveyance. Too, your father's important public position must be protected."

"Father is trying to find a way past the difficulties, Mama. And we're petitioning Jehovah."

Rachel leaned back wearily against her pillows. Her hand loosened its grip on Elhanan's. "All that is good, of course, Son. Yet even if Jehovah should provide healing now, at some time future we'll need a family tomb. It's wise to provide today for that sure tomorrow, whenever it may come." She smiled and patted Elhanan's arm. "King Solomon urged us toward wise provision ahead of time, didn't he? As in the proverb that directs us to be like the ant that spends its summer preparing for winter."

Elhanan's lower lip quivered. "Neither King Solomon nor the ants had a mother who was ill!" Unable to say more, the boy hurriedly left the bedroom.

That evening both father and son found it difficult to go into the garden for their usual restful time together after supper. Rachel was too weak to be moved from her bed. Elhanan was only able to endure the changed atmosphere of the garden by concentrating upon the fish in the pond and upon Tsar. He was thankful for the task of keeping the little goat out of the new-cut tomb while she frolicked. After defeating one of her attempts to enter the forbidden space, Elhanan at last voiced his heart's overwhelming concern.

"Father, have you discovered a way for us to take Mother to Jesus?"

Joseph sighed heavily. "None at all, Son. Instead, the difficulties multiply apace. It's reported that the crowds following the Nazarene are getting larger and more demanding. A person who is seriously ill could be worsened, injured, or even killed in the crush. As for the Sanhedrin, indeed also for most of those in any kind of leadership among our people, antagonism toward the Healer is mounting day by day. The bitter feeling voiced against him is indescribable."

Elhanan was glad for the garden's darkness, which hid the frustration and disappointment he felt must show on his face.

Then the quiet, dark garden came alive with sound and light. Tobias charged through the gate from the street, waving his small oil lamp, peering about, and calling. "Master! Master Joseph! News! I bring good news!"

"Here, Tobias. Elhanan and I are here. The bench had to be moved for the stonecutter's project. What's your news?"

Tobias, his chest heaving, came to a halt. "Leah sent me to the marketplace . . . late, since she'd forgotten several ingredients for upcoming meals."

"Take time to catch your breath, Tobias. Running can't be wise at your age. Ah. That's better. Now. What is it you've learned at

this late hour in the marketplace? I wonder you were able to find any merchants still at their business."

"Indeed it was difficult. So many stalls were closed that I had to range nearly to the Roman sector. That's why, and where, I came upon this night's excitement."

"Ah, so it involves the Romans?" Joseph prompted.

"Yes. A group of mounted soldiers came into the street where I sought to make Leah's purchases. The horses were badly lathered, and the group was headed toward the Fortress Antonia."

"And what did they do, Tobias?"

"They did nothing. It's what, or *who* rather, they had with them that's important. The riders were holding their mounts to a walk because of three prisoners, chained, being brought along at the rear."

"But that's not unusual, Uncle Tobias," Elhanan protested. "It's a common sight in the City."

"Not so, boy, as you'll hear if you let me finish my tale. The late-closing section of the marketplace where I was bargaining was full of others doing similar business. When the Romans came into view, a few rowdies who'd been sampling the wine merchant's wares staggered into the street to taunt the Romans. I feared for their safety, let me tell you! But to the surprise of all of us who were watching, the Roman commander halted his group. Then he asked the troublemakers to let them pass. Here are his words, Master—' . . . in view of the fact that these are the thieves who have been plaguing your people!' "

"Captain Melzar!" breathed Elhanan. "It must have been he. That's why he's been riding the horses so hard and so late!"

"If those he captured really are the wretched, traitorous thieves keeping Jerusalem in an uproar—"

Tobias excitedly broke into Joseph's sentence. "They are the very ones indeed, Master. The Roman commander motioned his soldiers to bring the prisoners forward. Then he shouted to us, "Behold your master thief, Barabbas, and his henchmen!""

Joseph brought his hands together in a single, loud clap. "Wonderful! Wonderful news indeed, you bring, Tobias. By capturing Barabbas and his fellows, Melzar has freed Jerusalem from fearful hearts and pillaged homes."

The City's streets bore a lightened spirit because of the thieves' arrest. Elhanan's own day, however, was routine. Midweek school lessons were dull, his time of caring for the horses unexceptional, and his wages from Captain Melzar came via a messenger. But with his earnings in hand, the day brightened. He hurried to Laban's spot on the street, and at last he placed in the old vendor's hands his first payment toward the blue necklace.

"So, so, so! I wondered if our bargain would ever be sealed with a payment, Joseph's boy. I marvel that you've not found yet another distraction. Good, however, that it's not so, for my patience has worn thin. Many have stopped here at my table—stopped with gold in hand, and wanting to buy quality pieces. Yet the finest piece of all had to remain out of sight!"

"Your patience had every reason to wear thin, Laban. In fact, it should be in tatters by this time. I can only say that I thank you."

"Aye, aye, and I accept your thanks. Had you been older, my waiting would have ended long ago. But a boy, well, a boy must learn his way in this world, and there are many rough places along the path, eh?"

Elhanan nodded. He sensed something amiss in the vendor, and he grew concerned for the old man. Their relationship had lately been pressured over the blue beads. Yet even in that, the vendor's sharp-tongued exterior had poorly hidden his sensitive spirit. Elhanan squatted, putting him level with the seated vendor and able to look into his eyes. "Could it be that some roughness marks your own road today, Laban?"

The old man jerked his eyes from Elhanan's gaze and twisted his upper body away, putting exaggerated effort into reaching for something behind him. His voice when it came was a growl.

"What, what, what? Why should Laban feel roughness, eh, when there's been no smoothness—ever?"

Elhanan's heart contracted, recognizing the truth in Laban's words. He edged closer so the passersby couldn't hear. "But even a hard road has its harder places."

"Bah! What of it! Old fool that I am, I deserve the jarring. I should have had the sense to keep my place here, to deny the hope of something better."

"Hope for . . . ?"

Suddenly the vendor leaned across the table. His movement scattered items in every direction as he glared at Elhanan. "Aye, aye, aye. Mad hope for a shrunken leg to be made whole."

Elhanan gasped as he caught the meaning. "So you . . . you went to Jesus?"

"Went? Better to say tried to go. He ever moves about the City and the countryside. And the throng of followers! On ordinary days the City is crowded, but when the Nazarene appears, the streets become as the sea—filled with those pressing upon him."

"But you did try."

"Tried, indeed, but always the distance, or the crowd. Bah. What uselessness! Would I'd not wasted the time, hadn't taken myself away from my table here and its profits."

"I'm sorry; truly sorry. Jesus' healing power is real. I've seen it with my own eyes!"

"Aye, aye, aye. It seems so. Still, all cannot know healing. I should have realized that and not wasted effort. Should have been satisfied, instead, with this." Laban's gesture indicated his table, its contents of items for sale, and his own body.

Elhanan could think of nothing to say. He shifted uneasily.

"Well, Joseph's boy. Enough of this talk. See, see. You've distracted me from business! Many are passing . . . passing without a look at my table. Go now. Hie you home."

Elhanan rose and left quickly, glad for the release. And yet his thoughts were burdened as he passed on through the streets. He wished the crusty old vendor could have been healed. And didn't Laban's denied miracle also apply to Rachel's situation? Even if Joseph and Nicodemus could manage to transport her secretly, what of the distance, and the crowding Laban had described? Could Rachel in her weakness even survive such difficulties, however dedicated her helpers were in trying to overcome them?

Although following days found him still concerned for his mother and missing Amplias, there was little time to brood. Life's pace was quickening both at synagogue school and at home. Passover was drawing near. While he welcomed thoughts of those sacred days, Elhanan also shuddered to think of the great number of animals to be killed during that time of national cleansing from sin. He shamed himself for such girl-like feelings; yet somehow he couldn't help thinking that the bulls, lambs, and goats were much like Tsar—warmly alive.

It was good to have everything at the stables again on a regular schedule. And when Captain Melzar came to visit the horses, he told Elhanan of the efforts to capture Barabbas' robber band. His mouth set in a grim line as he spoke of the thieves' taunting boldness. They had reveled in their power to elude capture. The unsuccessful pursuit by Roman troops had emboldened them. The master thief had even flaunted his name, as if daring anyone to best him.

"He was devilishly clever, Elhanan. But he was human too. We pursued and pressured them every night, and finally he made a mistake. One of his band broke silence, and we made the capture. Not even the most wily fox can endlessly elude being trapped."

"My people prayed for your success, Captain. Our Passover will have added joy because the thieves were caught. His arrest means freedom from fears throughout the City."

Elhanan enjoyed seeing how quickly his earnings accumulated now that he didn't have to pay for unexpected distractions. He

would long remember the day he took the final payment to Laban. The old vendor greeted him gleefully.

"Well, well, well. The day has come for you, eh, Joseph's boy? The day old Laban gets his full payment—poor and low though it is—and you get the necklace of blue for your mother."

"Yes! But how did you know?"

"Know? How ever could I not know, at sight of the smile lodged there between your nose and your chin, eh? One would think your very teeth would fall out, the grin's so wide."

"It's a happy day indeed. And I know I owe you much more than this in my hand."

"Let's not have talk of owing now, Joseph's boy." Laban took the payment from Elhanan's hand and transferred it to his own leather purse in one smooth movement. Then while the boy fidgeted, shifting his weight from foot to foot, the vendor made an extremely slow, fumbling search through his various bags and bundles. His mutterings added to Elhanan's agony of waiting. "Hmmm . . . hm, hmmm. Now then, Laban, have you hid it from yourself, eh? Surely it's here somewhere. No. Tsk, tsk, tsk. Nor there . . ." Elhanan felt that he would burst with impatience. At last the vendor drew forth the necklace. The finely strung beads were even more beautiful than he re-membered. Their surface shone smoothly, and each bead con-tained lovely depths of color. Gently fingering the small orbs, he knew with a delighted lift of heart that the necklace was worth all his hours of work, the difficulties, and the waiting. He carefully re-wrapped the necklace in its creamy cloth and tucked it into the leather purse at his waist.

"Thank you, Laban. Thank you," Elhanan said quietly.

"Ah, well, well, well. You've a fine bargain indeed, and a fit gift for your mother. Tell her Laban the Vendor had a small part in her getting them, eh, Joseph's boy?"

"Yes, I'll surely tell her that." Then Elhanan moved on along the street toward home. His feet seemed not to walk at all, but rather to skim above the ground. His mind overflowed with imagined ways and times to present Rachel with his gift.

One day at work Elhanan told Captain Melzar of the rejoicing he heard in the streets as Jews spoke gratefully of Barabbas' capture.

"Thank you for telling me, Elhanan," Melzar replied. "I find it difficult to gauge your people's feelings. Your leaders who came scolded us for slow work."

"My father says that we Jews seem to prefer complaining over gratitude or praise. When reading of Moses in the wilderness, he points out how our forefathers grumbled throughout their journey to the Promised Land and how that spirit displeased Jehovah. We've changed little since then, I fear."

Melzar patted Elhanan on the shoulder. "You're not responsible for your people as a whole any more than I am for all Romans. Instead, we must let their negative characteristics warn us away from similar failures and encourage us to be individuals of a better sort."

That evening when Elhanan told his father of the conversation with Melzar, Joseph was silent for a moment. "Each encounter I have through you with this Roman captain makes me marvel more greatly, Son. The man himself seems exceptional. But his employing you strikes me as being even more exceptional."

"How, Father?"

"Numbers of our people work for our conquerors. But the positions they hold are necessity—yours is opportunity. I sensed something of its unusual quality when first you asked permission. But over these months I've come to feel there is a deeper meaning. When you began working at Melzar's stables, you entered a classroom that Jehovah prepared for you." Elhanan made no reply. He pondered Joseph's statement, his gaze locked on his father's face. "I believe the importance of your learning there has many parts. First, there's what you gain in practical things daily, both with horses and with a foreign people. Second, you're seeing local situations from two different national standpoints. But finally and most important, I've seen that you're more greatly valuing our own faith by contact with Gentiles. And now comes the question: what will you make of this special schooling?"

"Make of it?" queried Elhanan.

"Yes. Remember the question Jehovah posed to Moses: 'What is that in your hand?' God intends each thing that comes to our hand to be used in serving Him and others, as did Moses with his simple walking staff. As you go on working for Captain Melzar, consider possible future uses for what you learn."

Elhanan's mind went over his father's words again and again throughout the evening. What, indeed, was to come from this unusual experience that had been given into his hand?

The necklace so dearly bought for Rachel didn't have to stay in its hiding place long. The next day Elhanan discovered that Joseph had invited Nicodemus and Adina to join them for the evening meal. He had of course also asked that Pashura come, but she had refused.

The little group of friends happily partook of Leah's carefully prepared dishes and their own casual conversation. As the meal ended, Elhanan excused himself from the table and went to his room, where he retrieved his mother's gift from its hiding place. When he returned to the group and placed the little bundle in his mother's hands, she said nothing but only looked at him, puzzled. Then, as she lifted the necklace from its enclosing cloth, she gasped. "Elhanan! What beautiful, beautiful artistry in these beads! However could you manage—?"

Elhanan was held spellbound in the moment of his realized yearning.

"Our son, manfully, has not only found this gift himself but also purchased it with his own earnings," Joseph said.

Rachel's eyes filled with tears. "There are no words to express my heart. The necklace is . . . it means . . . it's so beautiful, so full of meaning!"

Elhanan at last regained command of his tongue. "I thought the beads like the color of your eyes, Mother. I couldn't not get them for you."

Joseph, smiling, moved toward his wife. "Well, come now, let me put the necklace where it belongs, eh?" He took the beads from her hand and slipped them carefully over her head. The blue spheres glowed warmly against her pale skin. "Ah, there. You were right, Elhanan. Look how perfectly eyes and necklace agree!"

The friends' conversation continued briefly, then Nicodemus and Adina took their leave. Leah immediately helped Rachel to her room. When the servant returned to clear the table, she tapped Elhanan on the shoulder. "Your mother would have a word with you before she sleeps, boy."

"Yes, Mother?" Elhanan asked softly as he entered the bedroom.

"I wanted only to try again to thank you. These," she touched the necklace caressingly where it still encircled her throat, "are more than beads, more even than a gift. They are within themselves a celebration, a colorful, carefully shaped expression of my blessed only child moving toward manhood. How greatly I treasure this gift from your heart!"

Elhanan knelt beside Rachel's bed and took one of her hands in both of his own. "My heart yearns to do so much more for you, Mother!"

Rachel's reply came on a weary, sighing breath. "That yearning, too, is a gift, my son. May it see fulfillment through petitions to Jehovah for His will to be done—in me, in your dear father, and in you." She spoke no more, but drew his encircling hands to her lips and kissed them.

"Good night, Mother," Elhanan whispered.

Melzar's horses again needed to be exercised because their night duties pursuing the robbers had ended. Elhanan was so grateful for that opportunity after having been denied it that he fumbled with saddles and bridles. At last, however, he rode Lux and led Flamma toward the exercise grounds. Both horses sensed and caught his eagerness as they went to their workout. Elhanan delighted in the living strength of each horse beneath him. He had the horses walk and trot, then took them on through gallops, low jumps, and racing turns around obstacles.

When they returned to the stable yard, he found Melzar at the stalls. The Roman's stance made it evident that something was amiss. Elhanan moved forward.

"Captain, is something wrong?"

As the Roman turned, the boy could read profound disturbance on his face. "No. That is, not here. Things concerning the horses are fine. I can see that they've done well on the exercise grounds. But away from here I have, as it were, experienced a hurdle that proves too much for me."

"A hurdle?"

"Yes. My mind fails in trying to leap it. Perhaps your—the Jewish perspective can be of help. Let the horses stand here a bit. You can stable them later. Come. We'll walk about the stable yard. Perhaps movement of body will aid thought."

Elhanan could not imagine anything capable of bringing Melzar to such evident unease of mind. Working for the Roman had allowed him to see many evidences of the captain's calm, clear thinking.

As they settled into a steady, slow pace around the stable yard, Melzar began to speak. "When we captured the thieves, we Romans and you Jews seemed to come closer to accord than I've seen in all my time here in Jerusalem." Elhanan nodded agreement. "But now a new gulf has opened between us. Once again I lack understanding."

Elhanan held his tongue, waiting for Melzar to continue.

"Thieves are a plague for everyone, and of course should be caught and punished. But when there has only been good . . . How can your people seek to punish such a person?" Melzar was staring hard at the stone paving under his feet.

Elhanan's heart sank. "You're speaking of the Nazarene called Jesus, aren't you?"

"Yes. He whose deeds have caused amazement in every quarter."

Melzar clasped his hands behind his back. "We're under tremendous pressure from the leaders of your people. They want the fellow arrested. What do you know of this man, Elhanan? Is he, somehow, dangerous?"

"Only as our religious leaders feel threatened by his popularity."

Melzar nodded. "Ah. Threatened. Yes, that would explain their bitter, frantic spirit. Yet as I've studied Jewish religion trying to familiarize myself with you among whom I live, I've learned that a main tenet of your beliefs is the coming of a God-man. And isn't that what the Nazarene claims to be?"

"Yes, our prophets have long foretold the coming of Messiah. But through the centuries of waiting many have falsely claimed that identity."

"Yet this Jesus must make all those before him seem as nothing! How could any other be as he is: of common stock, yet speaking great wisdom; unassuming in person, but with amazing powers."

Elhanan sighed. "These are the very questions that harry us."

"What of your father's mind in the matter? Has he reached a conclusion?"

"Most in the Council oppose the Nazarene, but my father and my uncle have become more and more convinced that the man . . . has . . . is that there is something special." Elhanan's reply sputtered to an end.

"Ah. It helps me to know that, Elhanan. Even from afar, I cannot view the man as ordinary. Yet now we're urged to take him prisoner—our prisoner, but really the victim of your people, his own people." A heavy silence fell, holding man and boy motionless with its weight. Melzar rose. "Enough of these ponderings. I must return to office matters, and you to your stable duties, lest you be late home."

Jesus—threatened with arrest! Jesus—the one who preached peace, whose power had given Amplias sight! Jesus—the one who might provide Rachel's healing! Caring for the horses provided Elhanan retreat into a cocoon of habit. The outer quietness let his thoughts skitter about, crashing repeatedly against hard-edged unknowables. The danger facing Jesus gripped Elhanan's heart. He carried that distracted spirit into the streets as he made his way toward home, and it grew worse throughout the evening as he noted his mother's increased paleness and frailty.

The night seemed endless. Elhanan slept and woke, slept and woke. Whether asleep or awake, his spirit was troubled. When awake he stared into the darkness, his thoughts circling helplessly in his distress over Jesus' danger and worry for his mother. Surely there was something that could be done to reverse Rachel's condition! Surely Jehovah took pity upon her; surely He would answer the prayers he and his father were offering up day and night. Prayers. Jehovah's power. Slowly Elhanan's thoughts grew less scattered. They began to settle, until at last they focused upon a single point: he must plead for his mother's healing with some sign of his intense desire. But how? What could be done to strengthen his prayers' effectiveness with Jehovah? And then the answer came to him: sacrifice. Evidently he had need of forgiveness, perhaps for failing to tithe his earnings from Captain Melzar. The requirement to tithe applied only to those who were mature, but Jehovah might be displeased that Elhanan's heart lacked the love that would have moved him to give without being required to do so. He must demonstrate his repentance and earnestness by sacrifice. Yet he could think of nothing to give that would show how great his heart burden was. He finally fell into a deep sleep while going over and over the matter.

The garden's coolness seemed to carry extra blessing the next morning as Elhanan sleepily went outside to give Tsar freedom from her pen. He sat drinking in the stillness while the little goat cavorted. Then, after she'd had a reasonable length of time to roam, he reached out and caught her as she nibbled grass near his bench.

He hugged Tsar to his chest and moved toward her pen. She finished chewing a mouthful of grass, then turned her face up to Elhanan's and uttered a soft bleat. At the sound, the boy froze in place, staring down at the little goat. He felt as if an iron band had been pulled tight inside his chest, making it hard to breathe. Here it was—the answer to last night's mental searching! Tsar was a possession truly his own, and she was dear to him. She would be, therefore, a sacrifice in the fullest sense. But he frowned as he realized there was a problem. An animal taken to the temple for sacrifice must be without blemish. Tsar didn't qualify because her legs bore scars from Maachah's ropes.

But another thought quickly followed. He remembered his father's recent reading from the third book of Moses. If a person brought an imperfect animal to offer, the priest could evaluate it, sell it, and let the purchase price become the owner's sacrifice.

Tsar bleated and rubbed her nubby head against his chest. Again Elhanan felt the tightening in his chest, and sorrow at the thought of losing the little goat threatened to choke him. He made himself move; he ran to the slab-sided enclosure and hurriedly put Tsar inside it. Then he paused, trying to erase from his mind the special feeling of holding her in his arms; the trustful gaze of her eyes; the bleat that seemed an attempt to communicate. He drew a long, slow breath and straightened his shoulders. He must act and act quickly. If he hesitated, his affection for the little animal would prevent carrying out his decision. He hurried into the house to prepare for a difficult day.

Joseph left the house early, bound for his duties with the other men in the Sanhedrin. But how to avoid the watchful eyes of Uncle Tobias and Aunt Leah, Elhanan wondered. Then they, too, were distracted because his mother sent Tobias into the city on an errand, and Leah set about her household duties. He bade the women goodbye, careful to appear and sound as if he were on his way for a normal school day. Once outside, he drew a long, steadying breath, then took Tsar from her pen and carried her from the garden.

The way to the temple seemed both terribly long and terribly short. He tried hard to keep his attention on the people and activities in the streets around him; he dared not think either toward the temple or upon the small creature nestled contentedly in his arms.

Because of the early hour, the temple was not yet busy with worshipers. Elhanan chose the shortest line of those waiting before the priests. He looked ahead, craning to see the face of the priest toward whom they were moving. The man appeared to be both patient and businesslike.

And then they stood face to face. The priest's voice surprised Elhanan by its lightness, contrasting with the man's sturdy frame. "Yes, Son, what would you have?"

Elhanan's knees trembled, and he had trouble finding his voice. "I want . . . I have a . . . an offering."

"What would you give, and what is its purpose?"

"This . . . Ts . . . er . . . my . . . a goat. I give her . . . it . . . that my unintended sin might be forgiven and my prayer strengthened before Jehovah."

"The goat is yours to give?"

"Yes." As he spoke the simple word, Elhanan's mind was filled with memories of Tsar from the first moment he'd seen her struggling against Maachah's binding cords through all the days since, in which she had so enriched his life. He bit his lower lip, willing himself to go on. "She's not—she's not without blemish, sir." He showed the priest Tsar's feet, where the hair refused to grow because of scarring.

"Hm. I see. Give me the goat. I'll determine her valuation with those who buy; her price will then become your offering. And what is your name?"

"Elhanan, son of Joseph." Then he gave Tsar into the priest's hands, thankful that she neither struggled nor bleated.

"Your sacrifice is accepted as such, and you may pray as you feel led."

Unable to speak, Elhanan moved past the priest, searching out a spot as much apart as possible from other worshipers. His arm and chest where he'd carried Tsar felt so empty, so cold! His eyes moved upward, following the lines of the great, soaring columns to where they grew dark and indistinct at the top. He began to move his lips, searching for words that would express to Jehovah the agonized pleading of his heart.

When he left the temple, Elhanan battled awareness of Tsar's loss by reminding himself that Jehovah knew the reality of his repentance and of his sacrifice. He remembered a portion of a Scripture song of King David declaring that Jehovah would not despise a broken and a contrite heart. Surely no heart could be more broken than his in the loss of Tsar.

The remainder of the day seemed a thing distanced and unreal. Both in school and the stables he had the sensation of seeing and hearing himself as from a place removed. And yet he was thankful for the unreality, because it dulled his inward ache.

Returning home following the stable duties, he found his father there before him, seated alone in the garden. At first he was alarmed, thinking his mother must be worse. But Joseph assured him she was not, but rather seemed somewhat stronger. Relieved, the boy dropped down to sit on the ground.

"You seem weary this evening, Son. Were the horses difficult, or their owner displeased with your work?"

Elhanan sighed. "No, Father. I . . . It's nothing."

"Aren't you going to let Tsar out for her evening romp?"

"No, sir. I . . . uh . . . I can't."

"How's that? What prevents your doing so?"

"She's not . . . I mean, I . . ." Clasping his hands tightly together, Elhanan blurted out the story of taking Tsar to the temple. As his words faltered into silence, his father nodded slowly, without speaking. Then he drew himself up from leaning forward to listen.

"Well, then, since she's gone, I suggest that you take down the marble slabs that have marked her home. It seems to me her absence will be less painful without that reminder constantly before you."

"Yes, sir." Elhanan rose, glad to move away from his father's eyes. And handling the heavy slabs of marble would put strain on his arms, perhaps relieving some of that he felt inside. As he reached the pen his tightly held emotions demanded release, and he kicked the toe of his sandal against the nearest marble wall.

Baaa . . . baaa . . .

Elhanan jumped at the sound. Was he imagining things? He took a final step and leaned over the marble slab to look into the pen. Tsar! It was Tsar! She stood in the middle of the small enclosure, her head cocked to look up at him. He could only stare at the kid, shaking his head in confusion and disbelief.

Joseph's voice came from close behind him. "As you can see, there's no cause to destroy the pen after all. We know what trouble this one small creature can cause when she's running loose, don't we?"

"But Father, what . . . how?"

"The what is Tsar's return to her rightful home. The how is a certain temple priest's wisdom and friendship in sending a message to me about a purchase opportunity. But it's the why, my son, that's most important. Your willingness to sacrifice something so dear declares your heart to be warm and right toward Jehovah.

"Yes, but—"

"Your offering has been accepted, Elhanan. Tsar's blemishes made her unfit for the altar of sacrifice, but her purchase price, given to the temple, accomplished your purpose. It's simply that I had the opportunity to supply that price. I redeemed her, and I've chosen to return her to you."

"I don't know what to say—how to thank you!"

Joseph laid his hand on Elhanan's shoulder. "You needn't say anything. And I think it's time for you to tend to the subject of our discussion."

Chapter Eleven

The City's lightened spirits were apparent. There were multiple reasons. First, there was always a sense of expectancy in the Jewish sector at the beginning of a new year: perhaps it would bring their longed-for Messiah. Too, the month Abib itself, with its increasing warmth and greening vegetation was heartening. But crowning all was the excitement of its being Passover month. Jerusalem's population swelled as the great celebration approached. And now there was added the people's gratitude for the outlaws' capture. Elhanan felt personal pride in Captain Melzar's accomplishment.

While the larger world was marked by joy, Elhanan's private one continued to bear the strain of Rachel's illness. She seemed to be slipping ever lower. Thus, the new-cut tomb not only invaded their garden but it also loomed as a powerful threat to the fabric of their family. As he made his way toward home, the color, noise, and bustle of the Passover-crowded streets washed over him unheeded.

"Well, if it's not El*hay*nan come back to see me at last!"

At the sudden sound of Maachah's taunt, Elhanan's heart began to beat rapidly in his throat.

"Squeak, squeak! It's indeed the mouse El*hay*nan!" Maachah's jeer broke over Elhanan like rushing cold water. The bigger boy was leaning insolently against a wall, arms crossed over his chest.

"Good day, Maachah." Elhanan stopped and stood quietly facing his tormentor.

"Good day? Nice squeak, indeed, Mouse. But I'd like to hear it spoken from your knees. Down, Mouse, and beg me for passage."

"The street's not yours, Maachah."

"What, not mine? Of course it's mine! How dare a miserable, scrawny mouse squeak otherwise? Well, such a rodent must learn a hard lesson . . ." Maachah jerked away from the wall and lunged. Elhanan braced himself, recalling Junius' lessons. Maachah's bulk struck him full force, but he was ready. Hands, feet, and body responded smoothly. Maachah went down—hard. The bully's face flamed red, and his eyes glinted with fury as he jumped to his feet. He came at Elhanan again, this time with his fists flailing. Crouching low, Elhanan avoided the blows and twisted away. With an animal-like roar, Maachah made a third rushing attack. This time, with weight on the balls of his feet, Elhanan moved—first to the left, then to the right, thwarting the bigger boy's attempted capture. Maachah was breathing hard now, and he reached out toward Elhanan, his hands like claws. "Why, you wretched little . . ." He never finished the sentence. Elhanan heaved him into a twisting flight from which he crashed onto the cobbles. Elhanan stood panting, waiting for the next attack. It didn't come. Maachah stayed on the ground. "Enough! That's enough! You've *hurt* me. I'll . . . I'll tell my father . . ." Maachah's lip trembled as he spoke.

Elhanan stepped closer and stood over his fallen tormentor. Maachah cowered away from his approach. "Tell him indeed, Maachah. Tell him that for once you've received pain rather than causing it. Tell him . . . tell him that a mouse bit you." After a moment's silence Elhanan extended a hand to help Maachah to his feet. But the bigger boy rolled onto his side, away from the offered kindness. Shrugging, Elhanan spoke softly, yet demanding an answer. "So what of me as a mouse now? Will there still be a trap set here on evenings such as this?"

"Go away. Just go away. I . . . the . . . the street . . . the street will be open."

Elhanan took a step backward, but then he stopped and spoke again to his fallen enemy. "I'll go. But, first, what was it you called me? I don't believe you got my name right."

"You!"

"Say it, Maachah. *Ask* me to go away."

There was a moment of silence between the two. Then, "Go away, Mou . . . M . . . Elhanan. Please."

As Elhanan moved away from his fallen foe and continued his journey toward home, he felt less elation than surprise at his conquest. "Nothing!" he marveled. "He was all made up of nothing but a loud voice and cruelty toward any he thought to be helpless."

When he reached home, he halted just inside the gate, held by the sight before him. The tomb had been completed! Elhanan slowly took it all in: the opening cleared of debris and workmen's tools, and the great sealing stone now upright in its channel, standing to the right of the tomb's mouth. Pain clutched like a hard fist deep in Elhanan's stomach. Hatred for the tomb and its silent threat swept through him. He moved to Tsar's pen, gathered the little goat in his arms, and buried his face in her sun-warmed, curly coat. Only when she squirmed and bleated did he loose her for a run. He watched her listlessly, then returned her to the pen before he went into the house.

Elhanan battled the downward direction of his thoughts. The completed tomb was, after all, somehow a fulfillment of his mother's desires. Perhaps, then, it might even prove a benefit to her health.

When Joseph arrived it was evident that he, too, became dispirited by the tomb's completion. In silent communication of heart father and son spent the evening working with Tobias to return the garden to its familiar arrangement. Their efforts had a feverish quality. They took stone benches back to their original positions, collected even the tiniest scraps of the stonecutters' leavings, cleaned the fish pond, watered areas of grass flattened by construction materials, and arranged a number of Elhanan's lichen-covered rocks to soften the appearance of the tomb's raw opening. At last they completed their project and went wearily to their beds.

It seemed to Elhanan that he had barely closed his eyes before the household's sleep was shattered. First waking to the sound of frantic knocking, he then heard Leah and Tobias attempting to calm someone. All at once Elhanan recognized that third voice—Amplias! He moved then, all thought of sleep gone. He shrugged into his tunic and hurried toward the excited voices. Joseph and Rachel were a few steps ahead of him. The Roman boy stood on the doorstep, panting and disheveled.

"Amplias! Are you hurt? Here. Come in. Sit down. I'll bring you water."

Amplias did as he was told, gratefully sinking onto a stool. As he took the cup from Elhanan, his hand shook so badly that the water spilled.

"What is it, Amplias? What has happened to you?"

"Not to me—to *him*—to Jesus. He's been arrested! He was in Gethsemane's garden—praying, as he often does."

"Are you sure? How did you hear the news?" Joseph prompted.

"I was there, sir. At the garden's edge. There were several groups of us scattered about. He had asked us to pray. It grew late; it was hard to keep praying, and most of us fell asleep. Then suddenly the whole place came alive—torches, and spears, swords and shouting—a great group. They brought Jesus out of the garden and took him away!"

Elhanan turned to his father. "What will they do? What will happen to him now?"

Before Joseph could respond to his son's query, Amplias spoke again. "Something terrible, Elhanan. It can only be something terrible! If you could have been there! The hatred, the anger that surged toward him. It was not just in the harshness of their voices and the tension in their bodies. It was . . . it was their spirit . . . an air so thick I could smell it—taste it." Amplias paused, wiping sweat and tears from his face. "Only short days ago we entered the City and the people welcomed him as in triumph! We thought . . . it seemed . . ."

Joseph held up his hand, halting the flow of Amplias' speech. His voice was low, and he spoke slowly. "Aye. As in triumph. Cheers and rejoicing from the bystanders, eh?"

"Oh, yes, it was wonderful!" Amplias' eyes glowed at the memory. "There was such excitement all along through the streets. People were waving palm branches . . . throwing down pieces of clothing to soften the way for the foal he rode."

"As in triumph." Joseph rose from his stool, nodding his head gravely in response to Amplias' description.

"Did you know of this, Father?" Elhanan wondered that the incident had not been mentioned.

"Indeed, I knew and feared because of it. Then came more. The Nazarene denounced the moneychangers, drove them from the Temple. The incidents caused wave after exhausting wave of reaction in the Council. Waves that have now swept the Nazarene into arrest."

"But why? What?" Amplias protested.

"The air of triumph when Jesus came into Jerusalem was a bitter wind for the leaders of our people, since it clearly showed the Nazarene's favor and popularity. Then when he condemned the Temple practice of money exchange he threatened an established moneymaking system. Earlier charges of blasphemy against the Nazarene meant nothing to our Roman overlords. But these latest incidents give his enemies an effective weapon to use against Jesus." Joseph paused, looking keenly at Amplias. "Did he not seem like a king on that day of entry, Amplias?"

"Oh, yes. Like a king indeed!"

"It's undoubtedly that, the threat of kingly rivalry against Caesar, that was used to prod Rome into action."

"But Jesus doesn't bear himself proudly or speak words that exalt himself as an earthly ruler. I've been with him now for many weeks, day and night. He is all quietness, and humility, and . . . and serving. Serving the lowliest of people." Amplias' heart was evident in his ragged protest.

"Hatred has no clear sight, no calm thinking. It sees and hears only that which enflames."

Amplias' voice was tight with strain as he spoke again. "Everything has become like a wildfire!"

"Joseph, where will it end?" Rachel's face was white, her eyes enormous. "Will it . . . will it be able to destroy Jesus?"

"That's why I came," Amplias cried. "The spirit of the City is so changed, so terribly changed since that day of entry. All then gentle and warm is grown to a monstrous, blasting thing. The Council—you on the Council—must stop it!"

Joseph's head sank into his hands. "To stop it. That's what some few of us have been trying to do. Yet each time we manage to stamp out one flame another appears elsewhere. And the separate flames are growing, converging."

"Is there nothing more you can do?" Rachel spoke quietly, but her eyes were intense.

"Nicodemus and I have gone as far as we can in our opposition to the Council's general will. If we attempt anything further, we may be removed from our positions. Should that happen, both now and in the future the rabid Council members would be unopposed."

Silence held them as each wrestled inwardly. Then Rachel protested, "I can't believe what's happening. There are so many all through the land who attest to Jesus' power. As you can, Amplias."

"Aye, and in following him who gave me sighted eyes, I've gained a sighted heart, as well."

Joseph responded to the Roman boy. "And what has your heart come to see, Amplias?"

Amplias paused, knowing the enormity of what he was about to say. "It is not Jesus' *goodness* which is so hated. The cry of your people—those in the arrest and the condemning voices in the streets—had all to do with blasphemy. Their hatred is directed against his *God-ness*. Those of us near him find that charge to be not so much a horror as a—a confirming of what we've sensed, and heard and seen. The Master is surely more than mere man."

As Amplias' words ended, neither voice nor body of anyone in the little group could respond.

At last Amplias rose slowly from his place. Great weariness marked his voice. "I must go. I had hoped that one within the Council itself could persuade your leaders to free Jesus."

Elhanan went with Amplias out of the house. The sky was lightening toward dawn. At the gate the Roman boy stopped and turned to Elhanan. His hands busied themselves at his neck as he began to speak. "I do not know what you, or anyone anywhere in the land, believe of Jesus. But I do know what I believe. I have seen His God-ness—its reality and its power. And I am forsaking this god to follow Jesus with all of my heart." Amplias' hands came down from his neck and threw their contents against the stone wall. There was a small shattering sound. Amplias walked out through the gate. Elhanan looked down. Lying at his feet was a worn leather thong. Its odd-shaped pendant lay broken.

His mind was overwhelmed as he considered what Amplias had said and done. *God-ness.* If Amplias, a Roman, following and observing the Nazarene, was convinced, then prophecy . . . Jesus . . . But how? What? Why?

Throughout that day, joltingly begun, events followed one another so rapidly and with such increasing intensity that Elhanan felt as if he were on a runaway horse, plunging through thickening night. He accomplished that which was necessary in the various areas of his life, but a dreadful, breathless expectancy held sway. And questions swarmed like bees through his mind.

Why had Jesus made the foolhardy choice to enter the City in a kinglike procession?

Why hadn't he just taught against the Temple business practices instead of actually scourging the moneychangers?

Didn't his arrest end all hope of his being their blessed Messiah?

Why did Joseph and Uncle Nicodemus so steadfastly refuse to make known their growing belief in Jesus? Why wouldn't they do battle now for his release? Surely between them they could rally a powerful group of like-minded men in the Sanhedrin.

The recurring questions brought Elhanan to the most personal, miserable query of all. Was Joseph a coward? His father's strength, kindness, and wisdom had always made him a towering, respected figure for his son. And Joseph had consistently urged upon Elhanan the importance of courage as a part of manliness. Yet there was no courage in Joseph's determined secrecy and non-involvement in Jesus' behalf! The boy's heart ached with distress over what appeared to be his father's character failure.

How totally contrary was this to any Passover week he had ever known!

Elhanan was so torn that he wandered the streets. He wished desperately to find Amplias, yet he knew his friend's passage in the City would be even more frantically aimless than his own. Then suddenly all of nature echoed his inward turmoil in midday darkness and earthquake. While others around him ran, screamed, or beat their breasts in panic, Elhanan sheltered in a doorway. He was held motionless, viewing the mayhem as from a far-removed island of inexplicable calm.

When once again air and earth returned to normal, Elhanan went home to assure himself of his mother's well-being and her of his. Then he hurried to the Fortress Antonia, concerned for the horses' reactions to the strange events.

Captain Melzar stood near the well. His leather armor was partially unfastened, and his posture clearly communicated defeat. The face he turned toward Elhanan was ashen. The boy stopped in mid-stride. "Sir? What . . . what is it?"

Melzar lowered his head and shook it, as if to rid himself of its contents. "So you came, even after the disruption in sun and earth."

"I was afraid the horses might have plunged about and hurt themselves."

"Oddly, I found Lux and Flamma less panicked than we humans. Their calm has helped pull me back from the horror." Then, haltingly, Melzar gave his eyewitness description of Jesus' crucifixion between two thieves. As he listened, Elhanan felt a creeping cold engulf his body. Sickened by the picture created in his imagination, the boy's heart twisted painfully at the Roman's final statement. "He's gone now, Elhanan, but he was no mere man. He was more than a teacher, more than a healer. I fear for your people. They have demanded the death of one they should have . . . should have worshipped. The earth and the heavens knew—darkness at noon, and the earth heaving! What have your people . . . what have *we* done?" Elhanan's misery was beyond voice or thought. Melzar made sound that mingled groan and sigh, then he said quietly, "I've tended the horses. I had to do something, something normal, lest I drown in this sea of mystery and of wonder. Hie you home now, Elhanan. Perhaps your father has answers for what to me is only a vast chasm of sick uncertainty."

At home, the earlier quiet mystification had given way to frenetic activity. He found the two servants bustling about the garden, with Rachel directing their efforts from where she sat on a bench. Her face was white and drawn. Elhanan hurried to her. "What is it, Mother? Why are Aunt Leah and Uncle Tobias rushing about so?"

"We're readying our garden for . . . for a special visitor."

"Visitor?" Elhanan puzzled. "But why the garden? Isn't the house—?"

Rachel reached out, took her son's hand as he stood before her, and pulled him closer. Elhanan could see then that his mother's eyes were red from weeping. He slipped to his knees before her. "What is it, Mother? What's wrong? What trouble does this visitor—"

Rachel held up her hand to stem the flow of Elhanan's words. "The Nazarene. He's . . . he's dead, Elhanan."

Elhanan nodded. "I know. Captain Melzar told me of the crucifixion. But how does that—"

"Your father and Uncle Nicodemus have gone to Pilate."

"To Pilate! What can that—"

"They're asking permission to have Jesus' body. To bring it here, here to our tomb."

Elhanan's eyes swept toward the tomb, and he saw now what he'd not noticed before: Tobias and Leah's efforts focused upon the tomb and its immediate surroundings. He brought his gaze slowly back to his mother's face. Parent and child looked deep into each other's eyes.

"How brave they are, Elhanan! To approach the procurator with such a request. And more. If Pilate releases the body, your father and Uncle Nicodemus will suffer defilement by handling dead flesh. And now, of all times—Passover!"

Elhanan's response began on a whisper that reflected the impact of his mother's words upon him. "Brave! So he is willing to risk his reputation. Yes, it is brave, but too late!"

Rachel reached out and took Elhanan's hand. Her grasp was surprisingly strong.

"I hear disappointment and hurt in your voice, and I read troubled thoughts in your face, my son. All those emotions, all of those thoughts have been mine, as well, in these past hours. We must talk of it—of him, the Nazarene. For months, his person and his possible identity have occupied more and more of our attention. And now our hopes are all dashed. But, to be honest,

Elhanan, didn't some—no, *much*—of that hope have its source in our selfishness?"

"Selfishness, Mother?" Elhanan was jolted by the suggestion.

"Yes. Because as he rose in our estimation of him, our hopes for my healing rose as well, didn't they?"

Elhanan nodded reluctantly. Rachel touched his cheek. "Now we must move beyond earth-bound hope, while holding fast to the confidence that Jehovah does all things well. Your father has often read to us the prophet Jeremiah's assurance that Jehovah desires and acts for our peace and good."

Elhanan marveled at Rachel's determined faith in Jehovah. He bowed his head onto her knees.

"As for the greater disappointment, the death of one we were ready to recognize as our Messiah . . . At the least we must extend kindness by providing him a burial place. For he did much for us in his life, did he not?" Rachel stroked Elhanan's hair. "He healed your Roman friend of blindness. Surely, too, he showed us glimpses of what the Messiah may be and do when at last he does appear."

A troubling thought resurfaced in Elhanan's mind. He raised his head from Rachel's knees and looked up at her again. "Isn't it dangerous for Uncle Nicodemus and Father to ask for Jesus' body? One condemned by our leaders—executed. And . . . and the defilement!"

Rachel's voice quavered. "Yes, they face many threats, knowingly, yet risking all."

Sound and movement shattered the garden's quiet as the gate opened suddenly, and Tsar bleated from her pen at the disturbance. Joseph hurried inside and held the gate wide for those who followed. Elhanan recognized some of them as servants of Nicodemus. Tobias, Leah, Rachel, and Elhanan watched as the men carried in a bier upon which lay a linen-wrapped form. The scene swam in Elhanan's view, and sadness swept through him in a hot wave as he saw in his mind the gentle stranger in another garden. Several women entered the gate, cloaks wrapped tightly about them. Nicodemus came last, and he closed the gate firmly behind him.

The men set to work with quiet efficiency. The body was placed in the tomb, then masters and men joined in the effort to roll the great sealing stone along its channel to cover the opening. Joseph joined Rachel and Elhanan. For a time then everyone remained unmoving in the finality of the moment, staring silently at the newly closed tomb. The little group of unidentified women was the first to move; two went closer to the gravestone, while the rest huddled together, weeping softly, and then exited the garden. Elhanan touched his father's arm and nodded questioningly toward the remaining women. But Joseph held up his hand, signaling that they should be left alone.

Still in a silence heavy with sorrow, Nicodemus embraced Joseph, then he gathered his servants and departed. Joseph took Tobias' arm and led the old serving man away from the tomb. In the rays of the westering sun Elhanan could see his father's face was deeply etched with exhaustion, yet his eyes glowed. He stopped in front of Rachel and Elhanan at the bench.

"This day's work, I trust, will somehow compensate for days past, times in which cowardice held me prisoner. In Jesus' life I denied him; now in his death, although I do not understand his dying, I seek to honor him. So come now. It is the Passover. I cannot partake of it because I've been defiled by a dead body. But the rest of you must do so. This day's events have been strange in the extreme. Yet we must celebrate our people's escape from Egypt. And, remembering Jehovah's special choice and care of us in the past, we can renew our faith in His promise of yet a more glorious rescue through our Messiah."

Chapter Twelve

*T*he early-morning quietness of the Sabbath ended as two Roman soldiers suddenly burst through the garden gate. Joseph and Elhanan hurried from the house. They found the lead soldier looking around the garden with a scornful air. Elhanan glanced toward the tomb, concerned for the two women who had lingered there; but they were gone. Joseph approached the Romans, while Elhanan retrieved the loudly bleating Tsar from her pen, seeking to quiet her.

"May I ask your mission here? My name is Joseph; this is my home. And this day is our Passover Sabbath—a special time for peace, prayer, and rejoicing."

The soldiers turned in response to his father's voice, and Elhanan recognized one of them as Junius, whose instruction had enabled victory over Maachah. He started to speak a greeting, but Junius made a small signal warning him off. The burly soldier, who was obviously in charge, addressed Joseph roughly. "We're here under orders." He gestured toward the rock wall. "That's your tomb? And one called Jesus, from Nazareth, was buried in it yesterday?"

"Yes. But permission was granted me by Pontius Pilate. I can show you the parchment."

"We're not here to dispute your right to the body. We've been told to mark the tomb with the governor's seal and then to guard it."

"A military guard! But why?"

"The governor fears there may be those who try to rob the grave." The soldier snorted in derision. "Why anyone would bother I don't know. By all accounts the fellow had nothing worth stealing. But orders are orders."

Tsar had quieted when Elhanan took her from the pen. But all at once she uttered a loud bleat and wriggled in his arms. Junius' hulking companion scowled toward the sound. Elhanan clamped a silencing hand around Tsar's mouth. Father and son watched the two Romans attach Pilate's seal to the tomb and take up their positions in front of it. Then Elhanan re-settled Tsar in her pen before he and Joseph went slowly into the house together.

Back in his own room Elhanan's thoughts returned again and again to the garden outside. Despite his gratitude for Junius' instruction, Elhanan resented the military presence in their garden. It not only violated the enclosure's atmosphere; it also somehow seemed a crude insult against the one whose body lay behind the great sealing stone.

Elhanan struggled to bring his thoughts back into line with that befitting the Passover Sabbath—peaceful focus upon Jehovah's mighty character and His glorious past acts in behalf of His people Israel. Throughout the prior days of Passover observance he had experienced unusual exhilaration. Somehow each aspect of the familiar ceremonies had been fresh and stimulating. It was as if his mind had known a new light, his heart a new warmth, and he had been filled with yearning for the Messiah. Now within him were only the ashes of suddenly quenched passion. Oh, that Jesus had indeed been He! Surely none who came later could possibly fulfill in his person and in his power more prophetic indications found in the Scripture parchments! Yet just beyond the walls of his room lay the dead body of that same Jesus. The battle between exaltation, disappointment, and confusion filled Elhanan's entire being, making the day seem endless. At last came night's darkness. Elhanan sought his bed, eager for sleep's release from the day's heaviness.

The next morning Elhanan was jolted into wakefulness. Opening his eyes to deep darkness, he sensed that he had waked before others in the house. He tingled with a strange energy from head to foot. Unable to stay in bed, he jumped up, donned his tunic and sandals, and crept out of the house. He went immediately to Tsar's pen and smiled in relief to find her unharmed. He had feared for her because of Junius' rough companion. He took her from the pen and hugged the warm little body close for a moment, then put her on the ground. But Tsar didn't bounce off for her usual exploring. Instead she pressed against his legs, trembling. What could have happened to make her behave so? Anger surged in him. The Roman, after all, must have frightened or hurt her.

He crouched to comfort his pet and looked out into the predawn gloom of the garden. The stillness was profound, and yet suddenly the hairs on the back of his neck prickled. What was this? What was wrong? What had happened? Realization struck him with the power of a physical blow: the garden was empty! The soldiers were gone. Where? Why? Whatever could have caused them to leave their post? Their post: the tomb! Elhanan rose slowly until he stood upright, and his eyes widened as they focused on the wall of rock. He stared, unbelieving. The great stone rolled into place by the combined strength of several men now stood in its channel at the point from which it had begun its journey to seal the tomb! Had it happened just as the governor feared? Had grave robbers come and violated Jesus' burial place? Stolen his body? But to do so, they would have had to kill the soldiers, trained, armed members of the Roman military. Yet there were no signs of struggle, no crushed plants or trampled, torn plots of grass. In fact, the garden's morning freshness seemed richer than ever.

As Elhanan stood unmoving in his bewilderment, Tsar pushed harder against his legs. He picked up his pet and cradled her in his arms without taking his eyes from the tomb. She loosed a gentle bleat and tucked her head firmly against his chest. Her warm closeness emboldened him, and he moved slowly toward the open tomb, driven to search out its mystery. When he reached the mouth of the sepulcher and peered inside, there was no sign of disturbance. *But the burial cave was empty!* Elhanan stood stockstill. Not only had Tsar's trembling increased but his own body was gripped by contrasting waves of sensation—heat followed by cold, giving way to heat again, and then cold. His heart pounded. He began to move backward, one slow step at a time, with his legs threatening to give way at every step. As he put distance between himself and the tomb, Tsar's trembling and his own physical and emotional overwhelming lessened. He must get into the house and seek Joseph's help in this disturbing puzzle. But as he reached the pen and bent to put the goat inside, the garden gate opened with a crash. He jerked upright and whirled toward the gate, involuntarily squeezing the kid so much that she bleated in protest. Amplias stood in the open gateway. It was evident he had been running; his body gleamed with sweat, and he was gasping for breath. The eyes of the two boys locked, and both moved quickly to close the distance between them.

"What is it, Amplias?"

"May we sit? Now that I'm here, I fear my legs may collapse from the strain I've put upon them."

"Of course." Elhanan penned Tsar and led Amplias to the bench. Then, thinking of water for his friend, he turned toward the house. But Amplias caught his arm and held him fast.

"Your parents. Could you wake them?"

"Uh . . . I . . ."

"Please. I bring news. Important news. About . . . about that." As Amplias pointed toward the tomb, Elhanan again felt a prickle at the base of his scalp. He nodded his agreement and moved quickly toward the house. Going to the door of his parents' room, he called "Father. Mother."

"Yes, Elhanan? What is it?"

"Amplias has come again, Father. Running. He must have run across the whole City. He says he has important news about— I should tell you first . . . uh . . . the tomb is . . . it's empty!"

"Son, what? Go back to Amplias. Your mother and I will be there immediately."

Elhanan paused long enough to fill a cup with water from the ewer Leah kept filled. He carried it to Amplias, who drank thirstily. Joseph and Rachel emerged from the house, followed by the two servants; all four were straightening their hastily donned clothing. Sunrise softly touched the garden as the little group came together, and all stared at the sepulcher's yawning mouth.

"How? What?" Rachel inquired tearfully. "Have robbers indeed come?"

Amplias rose from the bench. The early sun lit his broad smile and shining eyes. Elhanan found his friend's expression to be as unnatural and puzzling as everything else about the morning's experience.

"No thieves have come here!"

"But what, then?" Joseph took a step toward the tomb, as if he would see for himself. Amplias' next words stopped him.

"None came to the tomb from outside except some women, earlier, bringing spices. But they found it—so." He gestured toward the dark opening.

"So then did the soldiers . . .?"

"The women saw the guards as their ways crossed out in the street. They were fleeing, terrified, babbling about being struck down. They've gone to plead their innocence before the governor. But the soldiers are of no concern in what happened here. Only Jesus himself."

"Jesus?" All of Joseph's household spoke the name as both question and exclamation.

"Yes. Jesus. Come forth from there." He swept his arm again to indicate the tomb. "And he walks among us again."

Stunned silence greeted Amplias' words. Day brightened around them, and birds grew full-throated with song.

Amplias shuffled his feet. "I know it's . . . it seems impossible to believe, but I assure you . . ."

Joseph moved toward the Roman boy; stood close, and took him by the shoulders. Looking full into his face, he said, "Amplias, what you speak is not impossible to believe. Rather, today marks a towering end of belief begun long before this day. Jesus' every word, his every act proclaimed his identity as our Messiah. At point after point he showed himself to be the fulfillment of prophecy."

"And now?" Rachel interjected.

"Now, and here, he has given reality to the ancient words of Job."

"Job, Father? He was no prophet."

"True, Elhanan. Yet he proclaimed an assurance that could only be true if death itself were conquered. He spoke of a *living* redeemer, seen face to face after his own dying. I long ago committed his wondrous words to memory: 'For I know that my redeemer liveth, and that he shall stand at the latter day upon the earth: and though after my skin worms destroy this body, yet in my flesh shall I see God: whom I shall see for myself, and my eyes shall behold. . . .' "

The focus of attention was so strong upon Joseph as he spoke that no one noticed a tall figure enter the still-open gate and approach them. They were startled by the unexpected sound of his voice.

"Elhanan?"

"Captain Melzar! How did you come here?"

"It's not difficult to find the home of a respected Councilor, Joseph by name. I had only to ask twice." He came to a stop some distance from the group, as if unsure of his welcome. Amplias began to retreat, but Elhanan caught his elbow and held him fast. Joseph quickly moved to meet the Roman captain, relieving the awkwardness.

"Captain, you're welcome here. My son has profited at your hands, not just by employment and training but through his acquaintance with you and your family, as well."

"I'm pleased to know that." Melzar spoke gravely. "That profiting, however, is not one-sided. In fact, his reflection of what you are as a family and as individuals gave me the boldness to come here."

"What may we do for you? If you would know of the guards, we learned only moments ago that they—"

"The soldiers came first to me when they fled your garden. Their story may sound wildly impossible to others. It does not seem so to me."

"No?" Joseph was incredulous.

"No. Rather, it's the capstone for all that has gone before. The man Jesus, from Nazareth, has been of interest to me for some time. Three days ago I witnessed something that was . . . that for me . . ."

"You speak of Jesus' death? His crucifixion?"

"Yes. Though I've had to attend many executions, this one was . . . different. There is no way to describe it. But I need not. It's the *meaning* of what happened there."

"You sensed something behind or through what you saw?"

A half smile appeared on Melzar's face. "No wonder you serve as a Councilor; your discernment is keen. Yes, I must speak of what happened here," Melzar touched his leather-girt chest, "through what happened on the hill of crosses."

"And that was?" Rachel queried, her eyes fixed on Melzar's face.

"A . . . a recognition. And a response—both mine." The Roman ran his fingers through his hair and squeezed his temples as if to free his thoughts. "I had heard of the Nazarene, had wondered at His powers. But to see what I saw! Roman punishment and execution is not . . . pleasant . . . to witness at any time. But in the case of Jesus, it went beyond cruelty. He received the most wretched treatment imaginable. Yet His . . . His utter *goodness* shone brighter and brighter through it all. But at the last, on the cross, not just His brightness but the limitlessness of His person smote my eyes, and my being."

"What was it you—" Again it was Rachel.

"The reality of His identity as the very source, not only of the light I saw in Him but also of life itself."

Joseph, his body rigid with intensity, moved a step closer to Melzar. "You're saying, then, that Jesus was—is—more than man?"

"Much more than man! In seeing Him die against the dark ugliness of the cross, I ached . . . here." Again Melzar touched his chest. "Ached at my own . . . my own darkness. I yearned to exchange it, somehow, to become as He was."

The little group, profoundly affected by Melzar's words, were silent and unmoving. At last Joseph spoke; his voice cracked with excitement.

"Exchange! Exchange of darkness for light, of sin for cleansing through the lamb! There it was. There *He* was: the very Passover lamb in human form, even as animals were dying for sin in the Temple!"

"I know little of your Temple lambs. But the man on that cross moved me to kneel. I could do no other. For truly this Jesus must be what He claimed to be—the Son of God."

"The Son of God!" The phrase came simultaneously from the lips of all Melzar's hearers.

"Ahhh!" Joseph's exclamation was ecstatic. "Isaiah so prophesied, though we failed to understand: 'unto us a son is given . . .' A son! His. Jehovah's Son. God in human flesh."

"But Joseph, what of his dying? What did . . . why . . .?" Rachel questioned.

"It's there, Beloved, it's all there in our prophet's words read endlessly through the years yet not understood: 'bruised for our iniquities . . . despised and rejected . . . wounded for our transgressions . . . he made his, his grave . . .' "

Joseph paused, looking toward the empty tomb. Then, with radiance in his eyes, his widespread arms moved slowly upward toward the shafts of dawn's light filtering through the trees. "It had to be so. The blood of calves and goats was only a token. In His perfect holiness, His utter completeness and power, only Jehovah Himself could be at once Priest and Lamb, making the perfect, cleansing sacrifice."

Joseph stopped, halted by the expression on Melzar's face. "Forgive me, Captain. I speak of things you've not had opportunity to know. And yet you've helped us to believe things we did not know. If you wish it, days future will let us—all of us together—search out the full meaning of our incomplete understanding."

Melzar and Amplias left the garden together. Joseph hurried away to share the news with Nicodemus, while Tobias and Leah went with light steps and youthful energy into the house to set about their duties. Rachel settled on the bench, and Elhanan allowed Tsar to roam the garden under his watchful eye. The little goat showed no signs of her earlier terror. Mother and son smiled often at one another, delightedly sharing the peace and beauty of their beloved garden. After Elhanan returned Tsar to her pen, Rachel motioned him to a seat beside her. She slipped her thin arm around him.

"Our garden is now richer, sweeter than ever before." Rachel spoke softly. "The difference has been made . . . there." Without looking, the boy knew she had indicated the tomb. "There where Jesus lay I, too, must lie. Perhaps soon. But now we know—we've seen—that death's power is broken. The sealing stone has been removed, its power shattered. As Jesus came forth from the tomb, so shall we. Our Messiah's kingdom was not of earth. But we shall share His kingdom in a far better place."

Elhanan marveled, not only in what his mother said but also at his changed response to talk of her death. The painful inner denials were gone. Looking toward the empty tomb, he saw that it was now warmed by the morning sunlight. So, too, had peace and assurance shone into his heart.

"What! Are you two still here in the garden?" Joseph hurried toward them. "Well, come now. Leah will be fairly bristling. It's long past time to break our fast. A new week lies before us, as does a new life. I'm eager to open the Scriptures together and rejoice over their fulfillment in Jesus, not of Nazareth but of Heaven. The Lord God Jehovah entered time and humanity, sacrificed Himself to satisfy the Law's demand of death. Our faith and forgiveness no longer depend upon bulls and goats, but upon the Lamb of God."

Rachel rose, smiling, to join her husband. "Oh yes, Joseph! May we *worship Him* on this the first day of the week—the day of dawning light for our hearts."